THE PHILOSOPHER CONVERSES WITH GOD

The Philosopher Converses with God

Michael H. Mitias

RESOURCE *Publications* · Eugene, Oregon

THE PHILOSOPHER CONVERSES WITH GOD

Resource Publications
An Imprint of Wipf and Stock Publishers
199 W. 8th Ave., Suite 3
Eugene, OR 97401

www.wipfandstock.com

PAPERBACK ISBN: 978-1-5326-9153-9
HARDCOVER ISBN: 978-1-5326-9154-6
EBOOK ISBN: 978-1-5326-9155-3

Manufactured in the U.S.A.   06/05/2019

Three questions steered the course of my life:

How should I live?
How should I love?
How should I die?

These questions are interrelated; they imply each other.
No one can be answered adequately
without first answering the question of god.

Contents

Note to the Reader

The terms "god," "infinite," "light," "fire," "absolute," "transcendent," "ground," and "sun" are used interchangeably in this novel.

Chapter One

The Deaf Fluteplayer

N o one knew his name, where he lived, whether or not he had relatives or friends, and as I discovered later on, whether or not anyone noticed him as he walked through the marketplace, the park, or a government building. A cynic would say that he was an anomaly: someone who lived in a cave, forest, desert, or on the fringe of human existence. But an optimist would characterize him as an alien or a stranger. As you know, these days, one does not have to be a foreigner, outsider, or extraterrestrial to be treated as an alien, for a person might be *alienated* by her own society, family, friends, culture, religion, or political establishment—that is, by her community!

Alienage is a relationship of separation or detachment from other people—*not only* politically, institutionally, or geographically but also socially, psychologically, and spiritually, because one can be *alien from herself!* An alien is an *other* and is treated as *an other* by the people who know her. She might even treat herself as such. She is treated as an other because she is different in the way she thinks, feels, looks, and acts. This difference is the source of the alienation. An alien does not share the community's religious, social, political, artistic, and cultural beliefs and values; consequently, her way of life is different. To use a popular expression, *she is not one of us!*

But although he was nameless to me and, I think, to the people who met him, nameless even after he left this world, and although he was treated as an alien by everyone who cast an eye on him, in fact, he was not an alien. At least to me and to the few people who knew him. I soon discovered that he was a highly sophisticated and accomplished human being and versatile in the art of human living—of what it means to be a human being and especially *how to live as one!* An inquisitive mind would certainly wonder:

1

"Why would such a person be treated as an alien? Who is the real alien, him or the community?" It is, I think, appropriate to say that he was an enigma, a person who was hard to understand or decipher. I shall not be too far amiss if I say that the story that shall unfold in the following pages is the story of an enigma!

And indeed, like a Rodin bronze sculpture seated serenely in a sphynx position in a museum of the human spirit in the city of the living, this nameless man sat cross-legged on an inflated stool, always in an erect posture, near the entrance of St. John The Divine cathedral at the intersection of E. Main Street and North Highland Avenue in Jackson, Tennessee every Sunday morning and played his flute until all the churchgoers, including the priest, left the church. It was obvious to me that he intended his music to please the ears of the faithful before and after they celebrated Holy Communion, the most sacred and most mystical moment of the Eastern Orthodox church religious service.

The instant he was left alone, he deflated his stool, folded it, and placed it in a white cotton sack. Then he put his flute and the benefaction basket in the same sack and hang it on his right shoulder as he sprinted to his bicycle, which he always parked at the southern side of the stairway that led to the main entrance of the cathedral. He always looked sideways before he mounted his bicycle and vanished into nowhere. It seems strange that so few members of the church were curious to know him or to care for him. What if he was homeless? Should a religious community, one devoted to the highest values of religion, not be interested in the homeless, the sick, the lonely, and the oppressed? I wonder.

To my eyes, this nameless fluteplayer was at least seventy-five years old. His head was covered with a panoply of white, thick hair, and his face was adorned with a long, white beard. His forehead was always lined with two deep furrows, an indication of a thoughtful, serious, and hardworking human being, one who had struggled with difficult problems and questions about his life or the life of someone dear to him. His eyes, which were protected by two thick eyebrows and punctuated with lines of white hair, always seemed oblivious to his audience and physical surroundings when he played his flute. They were constantly focused on a specific point—or should I say window—in the infinite space that coursed into his vision through North Highland Avenue.

Why that corner, and why that intense focus? I raise this rhetorical question only because it was clear to me that he did not recite or memorize his music, nor did he play it mechanically; on the contrary, he played it passionately, and he struggled when he played it. Most of the time, the furrows on his forehead were dotted with shining droplets of sweat, and sometimes, those droplets rolled down into the corners of his eyes and over his ruddy cheeks. I wondered whether he was aware of those droplets, even when they sometimes rolled down into the corners of his mouth. Any artistically sensitive artist would say that he was creating his music as he was playing it. She would also add that he was under a special spell or inspiration in this creative act. I am certain, without a shred of doubt, that he was sucking the nectar of his inspiration from the breast of the infinite. Where else can one derive the vision, power, and wisdom to transform the stuff of non-being into one of the most significant forms of being—namely, beauty? Alas! Was he in the habit of drinking this nectar when he played his music? Was it the Holy Communion he took every Sunday morning at St. John The Divine cathedral? Was this communion his rendezvous with the infinite? Can there be any other source of the creative act in art, philosophy, science, and human life in general? I do not know. But I do know that the music I heard every Sunday morning near the entrance of St. John The Divine cathedral flowed from his flute the way the sublime flows from the bosom of beauty and the way happiness flows from the bosom of love.

The fluteplayer piqued my interest even in his appearance and the way he conducted himself as an entertainer of the congregation of that dignified cathedral. His music was neither worldly nor interesting; it was haunting, transportive, captivating. It swept me into a world that transcended the ordinary world of beauty, pleasure, or even happiness. I did no hear it with my ear or even with my mind; I heard it with the whole of my being. It captured the totality of my attention and held me in its world until the end! I cannot describe this world because it is essentially indescribable, yet delicious, uplifting, joyful!

Why did this fluteplayer play this kind of music to a church congregation, and to the congregation of that church in particular, if he did not assume—or hope—that they would receive it as a gift the same way they received Holy Communion every Sunday morning as a gift? Why would a stranger offer such a gift? Why would he offer his heart as a gift to that congregation? A gift is something we give to someone or to a group as an expression of affection—of gratitude, love, appreciation, or friendship. But the gift this nameless stranger offered was different, different from the kinds of gifts people usually offer in our society. He was a stranger, after all, but a stranger who offered his heart as a gift! Now you can see why I venture to characterize this man as an enigma!

3

The people in whose hearts the flame of the spirit kindles are few, indeed very few. This is why a person like me, who has long been in search of another human being who is smitten with the fire of the infinite, would be anxious to come close to an alien like the fluteplayer, to breathe the air he breathes, to watch the sunset with his eyes, smell the roses with his nose, gaze into his eyes, stroll in the garden of his soul once in a while, see the world and its meaning from his standpoint, and feel the rhythm of the universe from the pulse of his heart. And I would be more anxious to sit next to him in Liberty Garden and have a conversation about his encounter with the infinite and his understanding of the meaning of human life and destiny.

This fluteplayer, this alien, always wore a grey, thick, and fuzzy tunic made of felt during his recitals in the open space of St. John The Divine cathedral. I am almost certain that the ancient desert hermits wore this kind of tunic. According to a story I read in one of my grandfather's books when I was a teenager, those hermits wore such a tunic mainly because it was ghastly and prickly. It symbolized rejection of worldly glory and commitment to a spiritual way of life. It also symbolized the transience and futility of worldly pleasures, on the one hand, and the absolute worth and permanence of spiritual pleasures, on the other.

The point of this symbol was to keep one's emotions and desires under the rule of reason. Some of the zealot hermits practiced different ways of self-torture, mainly to convince god that they were sincere in their rejection of the mortal world and their absolute devotion to his word. I am not sure whether this story is a myth, but the tunic this fluteplayer wore seemed to lend some credibility to it. However, what struck me as strange was that his pants were made of the same fabric as his tunic. An artist would, I think, say he looked like a Michelangelo sculpture playing the flute, but a philosopher, one endowed with a keen aesthetic eye, would certainly notice a contrast between the paleness and ghastliness that oozed out of his appearance and the flame of life that emanated from his warm and ruddy face when he played his music.

The former element of this contrast refers to the material dimension of human nature and the latter to its spiritual dimension. The former is the material basis of human life, and the latter is its spiritual basis. The former refers to the realm of necessity, and the latter to that of freedom. The former represents transience, and the latter represents permanence. This multivalent contrast perhaps symbolizes the dual essence of our humanity; human beings belong to two realms—the first is the realm of the spirit and the second is the realm of nature. They belong to the former in virtue of their humanity—or mind—and they belong to the latter in virtue of their body. But these two dimensions coexist and interpenetrate each other in a mysterious way. This mystery has baffled the human mind ever since people became conscious of themselves and wondered about the identity and the meaning of human life and destiny. I find it strange that many people today who are enamored by contemporary science and technology seem to overlook this most essential aspect of human nature.

Was this fluteplayer conscious of this duality? Did he conduct himself the way he did because his public behavior was a true expression, or objectification, of the way he thought, felt, and willed? Because he viewed himself as a follower of the ancient desert hermits? Or because he wished to remind his audience that worshipping god is not *a function* Christians should perform for one or two hours every Sunday morning but *a way of life*?

Although the first two possibilities are palpable and to some extent cogent, and the third is likely closer to the truth, I tend to think that he was neither aware nor interested in this contrast or in its symbolic signification, for it was obvious that in all of his recitals, he was totally absorbed in the creation of his music, not to mention the fact that he was also totally oblivious to his surroundings. His music was a flame of spiritual depth! I tend to think that, for him, one's faith should originate from the standpoint of god, the true god, and that one lives from this standpoint when she designs her life-project with the understanding that god is not only the source of the universe but also the moving power of her life and everything that happens around her. That he is immanent in the universe he created, and that without this immanence, the world would collapse into nothing.

I here assume that religious worship, in the way it is understood by the majority of religions, consists of two elements: *reverence*—a feeling of deep respect, appreciation, and awe for god as the creator and sustainer of the universe and human life—and *devotion*, which is loyalty to the beliefs, values, and laws that arise from a reasonable understanding of god's nature. Reducing worship to a formal celebration for a few hours a week does not only constrict but also impoverishes its meaning. It reduces the religious experience to a function the "faithful" perform on certain occasions. The more serious pitfall is that it idolizes god the way societies did during the early period of human civilization, and perhaps more importantly, it *formalizes* and, in many cases *commodifies* the religious experience.

5

But the religious experience cannot be formalized or commodified. *Worship is a form of religious experience.* When we formalize it, we reduce it to a commodity, and we reduce it to a commodity when define it by rules, norms, rituals, and conditions. The religious establishment, which formalizes the religious experience, also administers it and makes certain that its prescriptions are enforced. In a way, the religious establishment packages the event of worship and wraps it with attractive promises and desirable expectations such as social events, educational programs, the attainment of immortality, social acceptability, or eternal happiness. A member of the religious community is said to worship god when she attends church on Sunday morning and sometimes evening; when she prays, sings, kneels, and draws the sign of the cross now and then; and when she listens to the sermon and receives Holy Communion. Whether she gossips with her eyes or verbally whispers with a family member or a friend during the service; whether she thinks about a nagging problem at home, in the workplace, or with her friends; whether she is having a fit of anger, envy, or hate because she sees a member of the community she abhors sitting in a pew in front of her; or whether, for some reason, she happens to be bored, it does not matter in her understanding of worship. What matters is that she goes through the *formality* of worshipping—that is, of observing the prescribed ritual of worship.

Does this churchgoer know that at this kind of event, she stands before god? Does she know who or what god is and what it means to stand before him? She might feel a kind of obligation to attend church, assuming that there is no difference between attending church and worshipping god, *but what is the source of this obligation?* I raise these questions only to underscore the point that we cannot package religious worship, mainly because it is an event that takes place between the individual and god, because it is a spiritual event, and because its content and method of expression cannot be described or prescribed! Worship originates voluntarily from the human or religious heart, according to the individual's understanding of god and the kind of relationship she has with him. To be meaningful, worship should be an experience of spiritual growth and development, not a function among the many social, political, professional, cultural, and personal functions we usually perform in the course of daily living.

For the fluteplayer, true worship was a *way of life,* one founded in respect for, devotion to, appreciation, and acknowledgement of god's absolute power, wisdom, and goodness in the world. We are faithful inasmuch as our daily activities, regardless of whether they are at home, school, the work-place, social occasions, or the pursuit of our life-project, *reflect* or *shine* with reverence for god. But unfortunately, the majority of people who claim to be religious do not usually worship god, not merely because they reduce this "worship" to a function defined by the religious establishment—which often seems to be concerned with its own survival more than the *spiritual survival* of the community—but also and perhaps primarily because they hardly live according to beliefs and values that arise from god's being. What was the loudest call of the ancient prophets to their people but a call to live according to the word of god, namely, those beliefs and values? What was the most important sermon of the religious reformers but a plea to live, spurred on by a feeling of reverence and devotion to god? What was the most important exhortation of Socrates to the Athenians but a plea to care for their souls? What was the cry of the existentialists in the nineteenth and twentieth centuries but a cry for the urgent need to lead an authentic life—to be true to ourselves as human beings?

How can we be true to ourselves or care for our souls if we do not live according to the beliefs and values that originate from the depth of our humanity? A life that does not flow from these beliefs and values does not recognize god as a being worth worshipping. Oh, goodness! Do we call a human being "good" because she acts dutifully, or because her act originates freely from a good heart or will? Is possession of a good heart not what makes her a good human being? Similarly, is possession of a religious heart not what makes a person truly religious? But how can such a heart be religious only on certain hours, days, now and then, or *on demand*? Again, what is the use of going to church, of going through the ritual of worship, if we do not revere god in everything we do? If we do not know what it means to revere god?

I am inclined to think that if worshipping god is to be understood in terms of reverence and devotion to him, then worship should originate from the heart and mind of the faithful, not from the church or any other kind of religious establishment. This assumes that god does not need reverence and has not asked for it. On the contrary, worship is a human need. It originates from a heart that feels god's presence, power, and creative wisdom in the cosmic process and the history of human civilization, from a heart that knows what it means for god to be the source of the universe and the human flame that kindles that heart.

"Is this your view of worship or the view of the fluteplayer?" an imaginary critic, who had been following my train of thought conscientiously, now asked.

"I cannot attribute this view directly to him," I answered, "although I endorse it wholeheartedly, but I can say that it is an extrapolation of my understanding of the fluteplayer's behavior, from the kind of music he played at the cathedral, from the impact this music had on me, and especially from facts I discovered about him later on. Some of these facts are included in the following pages."

"What kind of impact did it have on you?"

"His music was aesthetically beautiful; it rivaled in its depth, sublimity, and loftiness the music you hear during liturgy every Sunday morning in the Christian churches throughout the world. It is, I think, difficult for anyone who listens attentively to it not feel the passion that dominates its tones in their varying melodies. To not feel the fire that kindles in this passion and be smitten by the flames of this fire. To not know that this fire was aimed at the infinite—the radiance of the infinite. How can you remain indifferent to the warmth and power of this passion? How can you remain silent after you are carried on its wings to its destination and turn your eyes to its source? How can you remain the same person after you stand on *the edge of being* and gaze into the boundlessness and exuberance of its infinity? What if, when you are standing on that edge, a finger touches your forefinger the way Adam's finger was touched by the finger of god in the Sistine Chapel? How would you feel? Can you comprehend what you feel? Is longing for the infinite not one of the strongest urges of human nature? What is the ultimate passion of the artist, the metaphysician, the cosmologist, and the mystic but a passion to be in the shining presence of the infinite—the ground?

"Please believe me if I tell you that listening to the music of this fluteplayer was an invitation to transcendence—to transcend the finite into the infinite, the visible into the invisible. Let me assure you that this is not an ordinary invitation, although it is extended to all human beings. An encounter with the infinite is not an ordinary encounter, either, although not many people aspire for it. I aver that you emerge from this kind of encounter with drops of sweat on your forehead and around your eyes and a storm of heartbeats raging in your chest, but that you also discover yourself laughing like a madman. You do not only discover the drops of sweat on your forehead and around your eyes, or yourself having a laughing fit; oh

8

no, you also discover that something miraculous has happened to you, to your inner self, to your identity as the individual you are.

"You discover that you do not anymore see, think, feel, think, and desire the way you did before. The beliefs that used to express indubitable truths and the opinions and values that were the solid foundation of your happiness lose their excellence. You begin to see with new eyes, hear with new ears, touch with a new tactility, and will with new desire. You even feel that you are lighter, as if your limbs are stronger and freer than they were, as if they have learned how to overcome the pull of gravity. The world that used to confront you as a mystery now stands before you as an open book, and the people who used to be strange, intimidating, and inscrutable now stand before you as they are without masks or makeup. But the most important change you notice is that instead of *fearing life*, now you *love* it.

"Fear of life?" my critic interjected with an expression of surprise on her face.

"Yes, the change you undergo is a change from fearing life to loving life."

"Can you explain this point?"

"I shall try."

"This is all I wish."

"The greatest enemy of the love of life is fear of adversity, for example, harm by others, sickness, bankruptcy, or natural disasters, and the greatest adversity is *death*. Let me shed some light on this type of fear. Whether it emerges in one's endeavor to complete high school education or university studies, to find a job and be a successful professional, to build a family and ensure that every one of its members grows and develops properly, to be a conscientious citizen and perform all their political duties, or to be in good standing in their social environment—yes, in all their endeavors to design and realize their life-projects, the majority, if not all, the ordinary people *proceed on the assumption that they should, no matter the cost, avoid adversity,* or at least to be ready to overcome it. They also believe *that they will not die,* as if they are immortal, not knowing, or at least not admitting in the privacy of their souls, that every day they live is a step closer to the last station of their lives.

"What if they reach this station? What if they stand at its door, and before moving in, reflect on the life they lived? What if they look into the mirror that hangs near the door of its entrance, and what if they see the wrinkles that cover their faces and necks, their sunken eyes, their shriveled lips, and the white hair that crowns their head? More importantly, what if they embrace the stream of their life and place it at the table of analysis and examine it? How would they evaluate it, and on the basis of what principles?

"Please, rehearse this scene in your mind and imagine that you, yes *you*, are standing at that table and ask yourself: to what extent does it reflect an adequate understanding of the purpose or meaning of human life? What does it mean to be a genuine human being? *To what extent was it justifiable?* Do you have any regrets? Do you have the courage to enter the door of that station with a smile on your face, not the smile of resignation—because life is dear, and no one wishes to leave it—but the smile of contentedness?

"How would you evaluate the truth or wisdom of the life-project you designed and the way you realized it? To what extent would it reflect a reasonable understanding of human nature, of the purpose of human life, of yourself, of what it means to be mortal, and the conditions under which you lived your life? Can you say it was *justifiable*? I have met a few people who confessed to me, when they reached the last station of their lives, that they did not regret the lives they lived, and that they were ready to die. Some of those people were religious, some were not. But most of the people I have met and who were in the same situation were angry, resentful, and remorseful about the lives they lived when they suddenly discovered that they reached the end of the line.

"With tears in their eyes, many of them mumbled expressions like, 'Life stinks;' 'Had I known it would be so short, I would have lived it differently!;' 'I wish I could have lived my life backward;' and 'I shall start a new life when I leave this hospital.' The kind of life most people live is based on fear of adversity—on a naïve understanding of the impulse to survive, and on the false assumption that they will not die. They do all they can to prolong their lives without knowing why. They theoretically admit that all human beings die, and that death befalls the neighbor, the stranger, the enemy, and the relative they do not like, *but not them!*

"The fear of adversity, and especially death, is often *repressed*, mainly because it is disturbing, depressing, confusing, and scary. Its repression into the depth of the unconscious is a defense mechanism against the disruption of the ordinary course of daily life. This mechanism is, I think, nourished by the impulse to survival, which is perhaps the strongest impulse in human nature. It is very difficult for human beings to pursue their life-projects if they are continually pricked by the fear of death or adversity. Preoccupation with this kind of fear stultifies the desire for life, the enthusiasm to plan future projects, and the attempt to enjoy life in the present moment. However, the tendency to repress this fear enables an individual to focus on the future with a reasonable measure of clarity, to confidently make future plans, and to feel hopeful about realizing them.

"But why should people fear adversity? Adversity is a fact of life. Human life is always a challenge, always an adventure. Moreover, is the fear of death *justifiable?* The desire for life and the fear of losing it is justifiable, because life is an intrinsic good, but *is the fear of death justifiable?* What is death but the cessation of life, of feeling it? How can this event be painful or harmful? Do you feel pain when you go to sleep? Does a patient who is about to undergo a major surgery feel pain soon after she loses her consciousness to the anesthetic? But even if life is intrinsically good, and even if we prize it supremely, do we have an absolute, justifiable right to it? Can we justifiably claim such right? Alas! Is it not clear that perishing is king in the universe? Can anything in the universe escape its scythe? Does anyone who comes into existence and delights in celebrating the rite of living have a right to complain when it is time for her to leave? Should she not act on the firm assumption that she is finite, and that her time would soon come to an end? Having attended a party and enjoyed it profoundly, would you complain when it is time for you to leave? Do you not thank your host and leave contentedly? Is the logic of coming into the world and then leaving it different from the logic of coming into existence in general and leaving it?

"Although they are rhetorical, it is not, I think, easy to answer these questions clearly or with a reasonable degree of certainty, but I raise them to emphasize the idea that many people grow with the erroneous belief and feeling that they have a justifiable right to live forever. It would be nice—indeed wonderful—if human beings had this right, or if immortality was possible, but it is not! Could it be that this notion, or belief, is a main reason, if not *the* reason, why many people deny it? Cast a look at the different types of tombs, monuments, and memorials that punctuate the mosaic of human culture everywhere in the world. How many human beings, especially the rich, try to find the secret of immortality through magic or science? How many people beautify the dead and the event of death at funeral homes and ceremonies? How many a scientist, artist, philosopher, and social leader endeavor to become immortal through their works? How many religions promise their faithful with *eternal life*? Are these and similar practices not modes of denial? Of denying the reality of perishing, or at least of repressing one's consciousness of this reality? Having witnessed the spring and winter of her life, who does not see perishing with her eyes when she stands before the mirror of truth and gazes into the wrinkles that spread aggressively around her neck and face?

"But why should we repress fear of adversity in general and with death in particular? Why should we live as if we will not die? As if tomorrow will always be waiting for us the next morning? Living this way is a lie. How can we design and live a life-project erected on a lie? Is living on the basis of this lie why a large number of people feel surprised, and sometimes shocked, when the hand of death touches their shoulder, or when a calamity quakes the ground under their feet? There is no need for me to answer these questions. I raise them only to spotlight the *facticity* of adversity and death.

"Is it not possible to lead a meaningful life with the understanding that human life is short? Yes, it is possible; but is it easy? No, given the present structure of the institutions—family, workplace, law, technology, information, religion, education, and society—within which people live and seek their happiness. But what matters is that it is *in principle* possible, as the stoics argued about two thousand years ago. However, living from this knowledge, does not necessarily mean that in every decision we make, in every project we embark on, we remind ourselves that things might go wrong or that we shall die soon? In this context, living from the knowledge that life is short or that it is an adventure means *living from the standpoint* that our lives are *vulnerable,* and that we are *mortal.* We live from this standpoint when we think, feel, and will our actions from this standpoint. When we assume a reasonably calm attitude, not one of denial. When some adversity, or even death, befalls us. You see, we can control our ideas, emotions, and decision-making, at least to some extent, but we cannot control the actions of others and the events of nature.

"Can I stop an earthquake from destroying my house? Can I stop a malignant cancer from destroying my son or friend? Can I control a madman who assaults me with a gun? No. But I can control the emotional outburst that surges into my heart in any one of these situations. Remaining calm or acknowledging the devastation that wrecked my personal life by a force I cannot control does not necessarily mean that I am a heartless, unfeeling person, or that I do not care because I can express or live my sorrow rationally without denying or covering the fact that neither I nor anyone can change the course of natural events.

"Suppose someone very dear to me dies. What can I do about it? Revolt? To whom? Try to resurrect my friend from death? By what power? Build a monument to memorialize her? Who cares? What is its significance?

Eulogize her? Will this resurrect her from death? In short, can we, as human beings, influence the course of nature? But if we cannot, is it not wise to deal with situations of adversity or death rationally, realistically and, if possible, transform this death into a life-enhancing experience, one that can promote the well-being of those who suffer from adversity or death? I am inclined to think that assuming this rational, realistic attitude is an example spiritual humility.

"Now, I can say that the music of the fluteplayer, or should I say magician, did not only inspire me to think more constructively and more truthfully about the meaning of my existence but also enable me to feel the essence and power of beauty more deeply and make my practical decisions more wisely. Now I understand more adequately what used to be recalcitrant questions about nature, human nature, and especially their reason for being. Instead of seeing the universe as a cosmic process, I now see it as an emanation from the being of the ultimate; instead of seeing finitude and mortality as a threat, constriction, or depressing realization, I now see it as an aspect of natural and human existence. Instead of feeling an urge to belong to this or that community, I now feel an urge to be in the presence of the divine; instead of allowing myself to be afraid of death or adversity, I now live from the *standpoint of* the infinite.

"But the most important change that emerged from my encounter with the infinite relates to loneliness. I do not feel lonely anymore. How can you be lonely after you feel the touch of the divine hand? On the contrary, you feel at home, the home you have always desired from the depth of your being. You feel secure in this home. Neither adversity nor death can disturb your inner peace. Do not underestimate this feeling, please, because it is an inexhaustible source of confidence, hope, courage, and love."

"Am I correct in saying that you have been charmed by the music of the fluteplayer?" my critic said, a shade of impatience in her voice. "Has it brought about the kind of transformation you have just described?"

My response to this question was no more than a soft, positive smile.

"I wish you could see your eyes, your cheeks, your lips—yes, I wish you could see your face in the mirror of truth as you were speaking!" she added. She pulled a handkerchief from her handbag and wiped away the sweat that was rolling over my cheeks. She also wiped the saliva that was gradually accumulating in the corners of my mouth. "There you are!" she said with a loving smile. "You should feel better now!"

It was clear to me that it was time to end our conversation that evening.

"Can we resume our conversation tomorrow?" she asked abruptly, as if she was reading my mind.

"Of course! I would be very happy to continue our conversation. The temperature will be fair, and the sun will be shining tomorrow. Can we meet at the rotunda of Liberty Garden?"

"Excellent suggestion!" she said. My critic vanished from my presence that instant.

Frankly, I was baffled, dumbfounded. To this day, I do not know how she appeared to me, who she was, or how she vanished from my presence at the end of our conversation. I cannot say whether or not she was a phantom, an angel, a daemon, a projection of my imagination, or some kind of magician! At first, I thought she was a logically necessary critic, one I invoked in the course of my narrative, but then again, this critic seemed to assert herself as a real human being. How did this transformation happen?

"Who is she?" I asked myself. "I do not believe in miracles or magic, and yet, it seems that I am participating in the occurrence of an extraordinary happening. She cannot be a concoction of my mind because she conversed with me like a real human being would. Her objections and questions were not only reasonable but also philosophically perceptive."

I understand that some people might freak out of their wits when another human being—or any material object—undergoes a sudden transformation of identity before their eyes. And I understand the equal possibility that some people might suffer a disturbing shock if a human being were to suddenly vanish from their presence. But my situation was quite different; the transformation my critic underwent was not unbelievable. I was not only a witness but also a participant in this process. How can I doubt what I witness and what happens to me? I did not rule out the possibility that I might be wrong in my judgment, or that what seemed actual was in fact imaginary. But I decided to go through with my encounter with her—to see what it would like on the following day, and perhaps on the following days.

I have always refrained from making hasty judgments, no matter the complexity of the situations in which I found myself. Besides, my critic was kind, thoughtful, and certainly benign. There was no valid reason to be afraid of her or to stop conversing with her. I was convinced that I would discover her true identity sooner or later. Most of the time, a stoic attitude is a healthy, constructive attitude. This is the attitude I assumed in that strange and rather confusing situation.

Chapter Two

A God-Intoxicated Critic

M Y critic was waiting for me at the rotunda when I arrived at Liberty Garden on the following morning. This arcade was frequented by authors, artists, lovers, and sometimes ordinary people, too.

"Please, pardon me for digressing into the liberating power of the fluteplayer's music last night!" I said after I greeted her and sat at the bench opposite hers.

"There is no need for apologies. What you said is quite relevant to an adequate understanding of the phenomenon of worship and to the question of the meaning of human life. In fact, I am anxious to hear what you have to say about the transformative power of music. Your description of the fluteplayer—and especially the impact his music had on you—intrigued me. I understand your description of the kind of impact his music had on you. From an aesthetic point of view, your characterization of his music is, I think, both interesting and provocative. Can we continue our discussion of this subject?"

"By all means!"

"You seem to claim, at least implicitly, that his music is not only liberating but also *transportive*. That is, that it can transport the listener from the finite to the infinite, from the visible to the invisible. This kind of transport strikes me as an ontological jump in which one moves from the *mode of perceiving* something in a certain way to the *mode of being* in a certain way. It is one thing to perceive god touching Adam's finger in a painting but something else to *actually* touch that finger."

She went on. "In your description of your experience of the fluteplayer's music, you moved from your aesthetic experience of the music to an existential vision of the *presence* of the infinite in which you *stood in the presence of god*. Is there a demarcation line between perception and be-ing? You glided over the dynamics of this movement rather quickly without explaining it."

"Thank you for bringing this important distinction to my attention," I said. "Let me first say that in this kind of musical experience, it is impos-sible for the music to be transportive if it does not enable the listener to move from one state of being to a different or higher state. Otherwise, it would not be authentic, in the sense that it would originate from a genuine experience of the listener. There is a radical difference between reporting on the basis of hearsay and on the basis of direct experience. The first is not authentic, but the second is. The first is not necessarily transformative, even though it can be, but the second is, unless one consciously chooses to resist, or refuse, the possibility of change. This happens frequently. Do some people not know the truth but decline to act on it?

"But the crux of the question you have asked centers on *the how*, on *the possibility* of the transition from the mode of *perception* to the mode of *being* in this sort of experience. This movement happens by the seductive magic of the music the way the Pied Piper of Hamelin lured rats from their hiding places into the river by his music. But this kind of explanation is metaphorical and perhaps hard to accept. The explanation should, I think, focus on the magical, seductive power of the music, on the aspect that leads the listener to transition from the experience of the music in the mode of perception to the edge that connects the finite with the infinite.

"Let me at once say that the magical power of the artwork in general is that it embodies meaning. The experience of the artwork *as art* is an experi-ence of a dimension of meaning, regardless of whether it is moral, religious, social, metaphysical, or ideological in character. The domain of meaning is the domain of the values of truth, beauty, and goodness and their deriva-tives. As human beings, we do not only live in the world of natural objects, we also live in the world of values—that is, in the world of meaning. This world is as real as the world of natural objects. The first is physical and sen-suous, whereas the second is mental and spiritual. The world of meaning is the world of the human spirit. Although this world is centered in the body and does not exist anywhere else, it is as real as the body is. We do not miss the mark if we say that the body is the agent of the *spark* in virtue of which we are *human* beings. Whether in the workplace, school, church, the social domain, the garden, or even in the privacy of our inner selves, what moves us in what we do or seek *but* the pursuit of valuable, meaningful purpose?

The different types of meaning we realize in the course of daily lives are the basic elements of our humanity; physically, we live in the realm of nature, but spiritually, we live in the realm of meaning.

"The source of the magical power of artworks is the meaning they embody. Do we go to museums, concert halls, and theaters or read literary works of art if we do not hope, indeed *expect*, to have meaningful experiences? Is the experience of meaning less real than the experience of a natural object is? Of course not. In the experience of a work of art, for example, this painting, this dance, or this sculpture, when it streams into my eyes or ears as a sequence of sensuous impressions, images, or sounds, I make a transition from the object that I perceive with my senses to the world of meaning that *inheres* in the object of my perception.

"I say *inhere* because the meaning I seek in the work is neither physical nor sensuous but comes to life as a spiritual content in the experience I have of the object. It takes a special skill to experience the work of art *as art*. For example, I can look at *Mona Lisa* as a picture of a woman looking into in an indefinite space. In fact, this is what my eyes see when I look at the canvas; they cannot see anything else. But then, in experiencing it aesthetically, I move from seeing it merely as a woman to seeing it as a *world of meaning* that lurks behind and within the picture.

"Let us turn our attention to the kind of music that creates an experience of the infinite. The quality of infinity inheres in the musical work as a potentiality just as the capacity of thinking the idea of infinity inheres in mathematics or metaphysics inheres in the human mind as a potentiality. The capacity of the intellect to think or speculate metaphysically, mathematically, and logically and extend the domain of this thinking and speculation beyond its boundaries, which is indispensable to the activity of thinking, is inherent in the structure of the mind. Without this capacity, we cannot even assume the finitude of any object within our experience. Moreover, just as the metaphysician or the mathematician can extend her thinking to what lies beyond her given boundaries, the artist can, at the level of symbol or image, capture the infinity that lies beyond not only the finite things and events that make up the structure of the universe but also the universe itself. It can create an experience in which the imagination is able to shatter the walls of the finite and glide into what lies beyond it.

"The power that shatters these walls is *beauty*. Do we not acknowledge that beauty, and here I mean 'the beautiful' as such, is an inexhaustible source of beautiful forms? Cast a quick look at the realms of art, nature, and human life and focus your attention on such forms. What makes them *forms of beauty*? The infinite does not, spatially, exist 'after' or 'beyond' the finite; rather, it *is immanent* in it. We experience the finite in the infinite and the infinite in the finite. It is impossible for us to speak of anyone of these types of experience without assuming the reality of this immanence. It would be equally impossible to say that the mind can think the infinite, or that the capacity to think the infinite, is inherent in the mind, without assuming the validity of this assumption."

"But although it is a necessary condition for having an experience of the infinite itself," my critic interjected, "for the mind cannot undergo such an experience if it does not express the capacity to have it, it is not a sufficient condition; what factor or power enables it to move from the mode of perceiving infinity as a potential quality in a musical work to the mode of living it as an experience of the infinite itself?"

"This power is, as I have just indicated, the power of beauty. Let me explicate this answer in some detail. The beauty of an artwork emanates from the unity of the aesthetic qualities that inhere in the work and make it art. These qualities emerge and become real in the process of experiencing it aesthetically. In this process, what was potential becomes actual, and what was sensuous becomes spiritual. The artwork, which was material and existed for me as a physical object, loses its sensuous character and becomes a spiritual object, first, because it is experienced by my mind and becomes one of its constituents in the experience, and what exists in the mind cannot be physical, and second, because the aesthetic qualities that exist in the work as a potentiality emerge and become real in the experience. But the experience itself is not physical.

"What is especially important about this kind of experience is that although it is grounded in the artwork as a physical object and ceases to exist when it parts with it, it becomes one with the object during the experience. When I listen to Beethoven's *Ninth Symphony,* or when I am engrossed in an experience of da Vinci's *Mona Lisa,* I am one with the symphony or painting. I become a drop of musical or pictorial experience. This assumes that I cannot perceive two objects at the same time. Although I can be conscious of the peripheral, perceptual field or environment in which the object is enmeshed, I can only have a vague impression of this environment. This kind of *oneness with the object of perception* is a common experience. Am I aware of anything around me when I am writing a letter to my lover, to god, or to someone dear to me? Am I aware of anything around me when I am in a serious conversation like the one we are now having?"

My critic smiled but remained attentively silent.

"But unlike these and similar types of encounters," I went on, "the experience of an aesthetically rich work of art, for example, *Ninth Symphony*, Tolstoy's *The Death of Ivan Ilych*, Brancusi's *Bird in Flight*, and in this context, the music of the fluteplayer, the kind of beauty the work embodies is not the beauty of this or that object but the beauty that underlies this or that object: 'the beautiful,' as such. The beauty that shatters the walls of finitude and enables an individual to move from the finite into the infinite is the beauty that exists as a potentiality in the physical work and steps into reality in the aesthetic experience. The content of this experience is not an idea, image, or feeling but the radiance of the being of the infinite. This aspect is exactly what makes movement from the finite into the infinite possible.

"We should here remember a point I stressed earlier—that the magical effect of the beauty that shatters the walls of the finite stems from an artist's ability to embody, in her work, her own ontological experience of the infinite. The passion I felt in the fluteplayer's music came from his heart, and the fire that kindled that passion was the fire of the beauty that shattered the walls of the finite and enabled me to stretch my hand to the infinite for its warm touch. How can the artwork be an occasion of transition from the finite to the infinite if the artist herself has not felt the hand of the infinite?"

"Is the move from the finite to the infinite necessary or voluntary?" my critic asked with quizzical eyes.

"You can take the horse to the river against its will, but you cannot make it drink. Similarly, inasmuch as the music is beautiful, and inasmuch as the listener is a genuine appreciator of serious music, she should be able to *flow with its course to the end* and grasp the meaning that inheres in it. That is, she should be able to stop at the edge and look out over the infinite that stretches before her eyes as a boundless vista. Like the horse that stands at the bank of the river but has to decide whether to drink, the appreciator of the music who stands at edge can decide whether to move into the infinite. If she declines to make the move, she remains at the level of aestheticism, that is, at the level of mere aesthetic appreciation. But if she decides to make the move, she proceeds into an ontological encounter with the infinite.

"When you listen to a lecture, read a book, or receive wise advice from someone important, can anyone force you to act according to the truths you discover or receive therein? Acts of growing in knowledge or happiness are voluntary. In a personal letter, my mentor, who played a significant role in my moral and philosophical growth, confessed to me that, having advanced in years, he found it difficult to act on the new truths he had been discovering. It was not easy for him change his ways of living at that advanced age. But people might decline to act on newly discovered truths for ideological, religious, social, or psychological reasons, too."

"What if one makes a move into the infinite?" my critic asked. "What if she has a genuine encounter with it? Is she under *obligation* to act or change her life according to what she sees or learns in this encounter?"

"If she is a lover of truth, and if the impulse to lead an authentic life that originates from her heart is sharp and alive, she cannot, I think, dismiss the new truth she discovers in this encounter because what is at stake: nothing less than the worthiest possession she has. We might value certain beliefs, values, people, objects, or adventures—but our lives? We are always faced, at least silently, with the question of what the most important thing in our lives is—the pleasures and glories of the world *or* our lives. Can we be true to ourselves if we do not satiate what some might consider the most valuable craving in human nature, namely, an encounter with the infinite? No one can give a final answer to this question unless she first encounters the infinite, otherwise, her decision will not be based on genuine knowledge.

"Ironically, a large number of people in our society are not curious to know about the infinite much less encounter it. They are more interested in the finite, be it in the form of power, glory, pleasure, wealth, knowledge, fame, or professional success. They live as if the finite is all that exists. Consider the unusual but widespread preoccupation with outer space and space studies. Even this preoccupation, which gives the illusion of a cosmological interest, does not imply or reflect a serious interest in the infinite; those who are preoccupied with it tend to assume that the cosmos is within reach, scientifically or technologically speaking. They, moreover, assume that the human mind can grasp the power that is the ultimate source of the design and existence of the universe. I am skeptical about these assumptions.

"Please, do not think that I am opposed to such interest or studies. On the contrary, we should promote them in every way we can. But we should always remember that they revolve within and around the finite realm, because by its very essence, the scientific mind cannot comprehend the infinite. When it stands at the edge of the finite, it stands before a mystery, and before mystery, it stands in silence, because its logic and categories of thinking cannot transcend the finite. 'Concept' is the datum of this mode of thinking. The infinite defies conceptualization."

"But then," my critic interjected, "how does the music of the fluteplayer provide an occasion to encounter the infinite, as you have been arguing so far? What do you encounter there? How can you encounter a boundless and indescribable being?"

"Saying that the human mind cannot conceptually grasp the infinite is one thing, but claiming that it cannot encounter it is something else. We can never encounter the infinite as an object the way we encounter a tree or a mountain, and we can never refer to it as an object because no one, so far as I know, has reported an encounter with such an object. Therefore, the kind of encounter we have with the infinite is absolutely unique, different from any other type of encounter."

I noted that my critic was looking at me impatiently with a bewildered expression on her face. I ignored that expression.

"The encounter I had," I continued, "and now I am talking about my own encounter exclusively, because I cannot talk about the subjective experience of others, was a kind of presence. And the presence I experienced, because it was infinite in its radiance, was the *presence of effulgence*. And if I am to express myself metaphorically, it was *the presence of a blaze*. I felt it with every fiber of my being. I did not only see but also feel its infinite warmth, exuberance, truth, and grandeur. I felt and understood what I saw without knowing what I saw and understood; I felt I was my true self without knowing that I was a self; I felt this infinite radiance without seeing it; I felt an arm embracing me, not simply touching my finger or any part of my body; and I felt that this hand had emptied the self I was of its ideas, fears, and desires and filled it with infinite radiance instead.

"In this sort of experience, my capacities of thinking, willing, and feeling blended into one capacity, *not merely of knowing but of being in knowing and knowing in being*. I became one with the presence of the radiance that enveloped me. This presence, which I craved throughout my adult life, is not merely transformative and not merely transportive, but it is creative: I felt like I was recreated in a new image, the image of humanity, not as it is conceived by this or that philosopher, this or that educator, this or that legislator, this or that psychologist, or this or that theologian, but as it emanates from this radiant presence.

"I tend to think that this kind of transfiguration is what gives true lovers of the infinite the strength and courage to remain steadfast in living from the standpoint of their vision—to withstand the vicissitude of life; to frown upon the pettiness that plagues the majority of people; to live, enjoy, and cherish the present moment, regardless of whether it is pleasant or painful; and to say to such moment, 'Linger and forever linger!'

"I know—what I have just said might sound like gibberish if not downright outlandish. But please, be patient with me. Let me first clarify the distinction between presence and its source by means of two examples. First, focus your attention on the sun. We know the sun by means of its light, or rays. If we remove its light, the sun ceases to exist for us. Ordinarily, when the sun vanishes, for example, in the evening, its light vanishes with it. But what is the sun? Can we have a direct encounter with it? To our eyes, it is no more than a small, golden disk. Can we see anything else? If we stare at it for a long time, this disk blinds our eyes. But we say it is or must be hot—how do we know this *but* from the hot rays that emanate from it? Any statement we make about this disk, which we call sun, is derived by inference.

"Light emanates from the sun and signifies its presence, at least to us; it is not a sign or a symbol of this presence but an emanation from its being, and this emanation is an extension of this being, although it is not identical to it. And it is as real as the sun is—all of Earth's inhabitants can appreciate that. Thus, when the red disk sinks behind the farthest horizon, its light sinks with it. There might be some light after it sinks, but this is only because it has sunk from one's vantage point, not from the point of view of the totality of the region. Now, when I am in the light of the sun, I am in its presence and am enveloped by this presence. I cannot directly make any statement about the nature of the red disk, but I can do so indirectly, the way scientists usually do. But any statement I make about the light is a statement about the sun because light is an emanation from it. An emanation is a mode of presence.

"But the presence of the infinite surpasses in being and dignity the presence of light or any other object in the universe, including the universe itself. This infinity forbids the mind from making any statement about its essential nature and forbids it from having a direct encounter with it, or consequently, from comprehending its essence (remember, the human mind is finite). However, although this essence surpasses our capacity to encounter or comprehend it *directly*, we can have indirect encounters with its emanation as a presence, because it is an effluence of its being, just like light is an effluence of the being of the golden disk. The closer and deeper we move into this encounter, the more richly and profoundly we feel its being. This is possible because the infinite, in itself, is present in its emanation. The universe, as an order, is an emanation from the being of the infinite: nature or matter; life or living organisms; and consciousness or human beings.

"Although there is no need for me to discuss or justify the ontological dimensions of this emanation or their relationships to the infinite, it is important to remark that humanity is the closest dimension to the being of the infinite, and that this in virtue of its intellect, imagination, and capacity for self-consciousness. Neither the rock, nor the apple tree, nor the lion speaks the language of the human mind or communicates its ideas or aspirations, but by their dynamic existence and the *rationality* of this existence, they, too, express and reveal the presence of the infinite. What if I have a dialogue with a rock or a lion, assuming that they speak a human language? What if I ask them, 'Why do you exist?' or "Who created you?' What kind of answer would I get?

"'I am a finite being,' the rock would say. 'I cannot be the source of my existence,' the lion would say. They would go on: 'Assuming that I am, or can be, the source of my existence implies that I existed before I was created, which is impossible. It would also imply that I can change my nature at will, but I cannot. And it would, finally, imply that I am greater than I, but I am not. All you have to do to see the truth of what I am saying and behold my modest, diminutive place in the scheme of things. But although I am such a diminutive creature, my very existence points to a being that is greater than I am. Such a being exists because I exist, and it does not exist independently of me, because if it did, I would cease to exist. Therefore, I advise you to examine me and look for traces of this being within me; I am certain that it permeates the existence of all physical and living things that make up the structure of the universe.' In the view of the preceding exchange, the human encounter with the emanation of the infinite in all of its dimensions is, to my mind, the loftiest, worthiest experience human nature craves from the depth of its being. This craving is a craving for its source!"

"What you said in your account of your experience of the infinite is interesting, indeed intriguing," my critic said, "but I have a hunch that many philosophers, theologians, and ordinary people would reject your claim that an aesthetic experience can be an invitation to a transition from the finite to the infinite. Or that a human being can, by her individual effort, make such a transition. They would raise questions about the *objectivity* and justifiability of these claims. What do you think?"

"But is it not the essence of all value experiences to be subjective without necessarily being relative or idiosyncratic? For example, the experience of beauty in art, nature, and human life is subjective, but is it necessarily relative or idiosyncratic? Again, the experience of love is subjective, but is it not possible for a statement or expression of love to be objectively true and justifiable? Do we justify the truth of a scientific statement only on the basis of its correspondence to a mental state or belief, or *also* on the basis of the effects it produces? Do we judge a human being merely on the basis of what she thinks or feels or says about herself or *also* on the basis of the actions she performs or the kind of life she leads? Do her actions not reveal the kind of human being she is? Similarly, should we not judge a person who claims that she had an encounter with the infinite *only* on the basis of the claim she makes but *also* on the kind of life she leads? What if a person claims that she is a saint and logically convinces us that she is one, but she behaves like a villain or a thug? Can we believe such a person? Or, what if a person says nothing about herself, good or bad, but actually behaves like a saint, do we hesitate in viewing her as a saint? Well—"

"May I please ask you to postpone the discussion of this question? I have a more pressing concern," my critic intervened abruptly.

"Of course!"

"In your description of the fluteplayer's character, you alluded, rather briefly, to the phenomenon of worship. You seemed to imply that worshipping god should not be restricted to a one- or two-hour event on a certain day of the week but be performed, revealed, and expressed in all daily activities. You also seemed to imply that the life of the individual should be an event of worship. Am I correct in my observation?"

"Yes, you are."

"Not many philosophers or theologians discuss, much less advocate for, this conception of worship. Would you please explain, in some detail, what you mean by *worship* as a religious phenomenon?"

"I shall try," I said.

"This is all I expect."

"It is, I think, important to begin my explanation with a working definition of worship, for without such a definition, the explanation would be vitiated with vagueness, digressions, and mistakes. Clarity of propose and focus are essential to any meaningful dialogue. Moreover, the definition I shall propose will be brief and general. As far as I know, it will attract the approval of the majority of, if not all, theologians and philosophers because it is extrapolated from a phenomenological observation of the way human beings worship the ultimate (or god) in the majority of major religions of the world. This definition will, moreover, be based on my personal experience as a former active member of the Eastern Orthodox church. My aim is to treat worship as a *living* religious phenomenon, not merely as a philosophical conception."

"I welcome this approach," my critic said.

"Let me submit that 'worship' denotes an attitude or spiritual orientation that one assumes toward god as a being who is absolute in power, wisdom, and goodness; who created the universe; and who has a personal relationship with human beings. Without saying that he has this kind of relationship with human beings, worship would lose it meaning and relevance to the faithful. By 'attitude,' I mean an established way of thinking, feeling, and acting in the world. In this context, this kind of attitude means that one thinks, feels, and acts from the standpoint of her understanding of god. Next, to worship god means to revere him, and to revere means to love him, respect him, and show devotion to him. It also means to stand in *awe* before the majesty of his absoluteness. Worshippers generally attribute adjectives such as 'holy,' 'sacred,' and 'divine' to him to emphasize his absolute uniqueness and spiritual purity. The religious attitude is expressed in and through a certain communal ritual in which the faithful adore and express their love, respect, and devotion to god. Let me now discuss the assumptions, meanings, and implications of this general definition.

"We can, to begin, say that the purpose of worship is twofold: to revere god and to pray to him. Worship is, to a large extent, a communal event. The faithful gather as a community in a special building and worship god once a week, and on festive occasions, they do so more than once, often for about one or two hours. This event takes place as a ritual generally called liturgy (mass or service). The church building is consecrated, or designed, as a house of worship, as a place where people can stand in the presence of god. The act of consecration creates a line that makes a distinction between *sacred and secular spaces*. The interior of the church is a sacred space, whereas its exterior is a secular space. The first is sacred because god's presence to the faithful transforms it into a holy place; wherever god is present is a holy place. A corollary to this idea is the assumption that worship is a religious moment at its best because god's presence in it *is its reason for being*. In this moment, which defines 'the spiritual' as such, the faithful feel clean, purified. This is why many willingly prepare themselves for it by fasting, confessing, receiving forgiveness, taking baths, and refraining from using bad words or performing immoral acts before receiving Holy Communion.

Implied in this religious orientation is the belief that worshipping god in church expresses the essence of the religious moment: one is, or becomes, *religious* in the presence of god, and one experiences this presence in church on Sunday morning. It would be wrong for a person to stand before god in church with an evil or sinful heart, but ironically enough, it seems alright to entertain evil thoughts or intentions outside the church because the faithful assume, rightly or wrongly, that god is not present in the realm of nature or in secular space. When I was a boy, I used to watch my grandfather gulp a few long sips of cognac from a bottle that he always kept in the inner pocket of his jacket. Once, after he had taken a long drink, which was followed by an episode of coughing, I asked him, 'Why do you attend liturgy if you drink this way the moment you leave the church building?'

"'Oh, son,' he replied, 'I feel happy after I attend liturgy.' He paused for a few seconds and then added, 'Now, I can continue sinning until next Sunday. Then I shall confess to the priest again. I am sure he will grant me absolution. He always does. This way, I can have communion and glorify god and also have my cognac.' I wonder whether my grandfather treated the event of worship as a kind of spiritual urn for the purification of souls by the priest!

"I recount this personal experience only to stress that, at least at the level of practice, believers tend to view the church as a sacred place—a house of god. It is crucially important to point out that in this context, the phenomenon of worship, in its different dimensions, is determined by the religious establishment: the need to worship god, how one worships him, the consecration of the church building, and all of the practices and rites associated with it, even its justification. If we cast a general, investigative look at different religions and different denominations within religions, we readily discern a large assortment of conceptions and practices of worshipping god.

"One might be justified in making the inference that this phenomenon is a *human construct*. The articulation of this construct seems to depend on social, religious, political, and cultural factors. It is generally recognized that these factors change from one society to another and from one historical period to another. Does this mean that there cannot be one valid way of worshipping god? I wonder! Moreover, has any religious community consulted god to see whether he wished to be worshipped to begin with? Or perhaps whether or not he wished to be worshipped in *a certain way*? Again, I wonder!

"Although brief, the purpose of the preceding explanation is only to provide a basis for shedding as much light as possible on the fluteplayer's view that worshipping god should not be restricted to a formal ritual administered by religious professionals on a certain day. Rather, it should be reflected in the different activities that make up the structure of one's life."

"I am trying to follow your line of reasoning," my critic said.

"Now, let us ask, *before whom* do the faithful stand in the event of worship?" I asked her.

"Before god!" my critic replied enthusiastically, with puzzled eyes. "After all, god is the only object of worship. At least, this is what the majority of worshippers claim. Besides, you emphasized this point exactly."

"Yes, I did, but I did on behalf of the ordinary worshipper. Can I assume that you are such a worshipper?" I asked with an air of inquisitiveness in my voice, not only because I wished to know her personal identity but also her religious identity, if she had one.

"I am a religious person."

"Religious?" I retorted. Her answer was vague. The word "religious" has different connotations, I thought. Was she evading my question?

"Yes, the ideas you have been expounding are unsettling. I am not anymore certain what I should believe. You must be some siren who casts spells on his interlocutors and seduces them into new ways of feeling and thinking."

"Do I have this power, or does the truth of the ideas I am expounding have it?"

"I cannot see the difference between them. How can I, when the truth I discern comes from your mouth?"

I did not answer her question because I could not, so I remained silent. Both of us were thrown into a somewhat awkward moment.

"Well," I continued, trying to overcome the feeling of awkwardness, "the reason I raised this question on behalf of the ordinary worshipper is to *zero in on the anatomy* of the act of worship. Does the worshipper stand in this act before god the way she stands before a tree or a lion? Notice: the focus of my question is the *identity and mode of existence* of the object of worship. When I stand before a tree, for example, I see the object with my eyes. I can identify and describe it. In this case, my knowledge of the tree is based on my sensuous encounter with it. The tree I see is the basis of my knowledge of it as well as the basis of the truth or falsity of my knowledge."

"I understand your point," my critic said. "In the act of worship, and let me speak now in the first person, I stand before god as a being who is absolute in power, wisdom, and goodness; as a being who created the universe; and as a being who cares about his creations and with whom I can have a personal relationship. This being is not an ordinary object because he is infinite in every way you can imagine."

"How can a finite being like you stand before the infinite?" I asked. "How can you claim knowledge of his infinite essence, and more importantly, how can you worship such a being? I know what it means for one to love, respect, or revere a king, a scientist, or a sage, but how can one love, respect, or revere the infinite?"

"Indirectly!"

"How—indirectly? Can you explain what you mean by this answer?"

"On faith. As an Eastern Orthodox Christian, I believe that god is the infinite who is absolute in power, wisdom, and goodness, like you have just said. I also believe that he revealed himself in the person of Jesus Christ. I know god, and I worship him through Jesus. I stand before him during liturgy and feel his presence during the celebration of Holy Communion."

You have said so much in a few words," I said, awed.

"Have I?" she asked.

"Oh yes! In fact, those few words have provoked a bundle of questions in my mind. Can I raise some that are relevant to our discussion?"

"Yes."

"How do you know that the infinite has revealed himself in the person of a human being like Jesus Christ?"

"It is stated in the Bible. I believe that what the Bible says is true."

"What makes you believe that *what* the Bible says is true? Did you read it carefully, examine it critically in its religious and historical contexts, and then determine that what it says is true? Indubitably true? Or did you acquire your belief in the Bible the way people usually acquire language, tastes, desires, beliefs, values, and social behaviors? That is, in the process of growing up and existing within different institutions? Society, family, school, church, law, art, and the workplace? For example, did you become a believer in Christian doctrine by *practicing* the Christian way of life ever since you were a child, or *after* you matured intellectually, emotionally, socially, aesthetically, and scientifically? *After* you studied the bible, and *after* you studied the religious texts of other religions? I am trying to focus your attention on the source, or basis, of your belief that god has revealed himself in the person Jesus Christ."

I continued. "Now, what if one asks you, how does the infinite reveal itself in a finite being? Why did he choose Jesus over someone else? Was his character or teaching ability superior to that of the founders of other religions? Have you considered this question? Again, does the infinite exist in Jesus, or is it revealed in him as a teacher? There is a difference between revelation and being—between being one with god and being his messenger."

"I did not study the Bible the way you did, and I doubt that most of the faithful have studied it to that extent, either. Like everyone else, *I grew up as a Christian,* and I espouse the values and beliefs of Christianity. I understand these beliefs and values and live according to them. They are the ultimate source of my desires and actions. I am a Christian. This is my religious identity. I cannot conceive myself as having any other identity. I am a believer; it is difficult, and I think impossible, for me to deny or relinquish my way of thinking and feeling about god—"

"About god?" I snapped.

"Yes!"

"What do you conceive when you utter the words 'god' or when I mention his name in a sentence? For example, when I utter the word 'tree,' I conceive a general idea. This idea refers to any possible tree anywhere in the world. And when I utter 'Socrates,' I conceive a particular human being with specific physical and human features. What kind of idea do you conceive when I utter the word 'god?'"

"As I said before, I conceive a being who is absolute in power, wisdom, and goodness, a being who created the universe. This being is not indifferent to his creation but cares about it."

"This idea was first articulated by the church—correct?"

"By the founders of the church."

"Those founders were human beings like *you and me*—would you agree?" I emphasized the *like you* phrase to see if I could elicit some information about her personal identity.

"Certainly," she said.

"Would you also agree that the ideas human beings articulate, conceive, and create are derived from their experiences as finite beings? That because these ideas are derived from their experiences, that these experiences apply only to particular, finite objects? For example, although they cannot experience the *infinite in itself,* they can construct an idea of infinity based on their own experience of finite things. The idea of 'god' is general and can never be *truly descriptive* of what it is supposed to signify in the same way the idea of 'tree' can. For example, some metaphysicians say that the universe is infinite. How did they arrive at this concept of infinity? Have they experienced the infinite in the fullness of its being the way the botanist experiences the tree in the fulness of its being? No. Well then, what justifies their construction of the idea of infinity? We can certainly say that they arrive at the idea of infinity by experiencing the finite, and they can say that the finite points, by nature, to the existence of what lies beyond the finite. In other words, because the finite can be grasped by us, what lies beyond the finite must be infinite. And yet, if we ask these metaphysicians, 'What is this infinite?' the only answer they can provide is a silent smile! Would you agree with this line of reasoning?"

"I would."

"You say that the Christian concept of god was first articulated by the founders of the church. How did they arrive at the idea that god is absolute in power, wisdom, and goodness; that he created the universe; and that he cares about his creations? Did they stand before him—an infinite being—and directly examine his nature the way a biologist examines the nature of living cell under a microscope? Or did they arrive at it by reflecting on the nature of existence in general, human nature, and the kind of person Jesus was? Was this reflection not done from the standpoint of finite individuals who thrived in a particular social, cultural, and political environment?"

"I tend think that the latter is the correct answer."

"Now, would you agree that your conception of the god you worship in church on Sunday morning for about one hour is a construct of the human mind?"

My critic hesitated a little but then answered the question affirmatively but reluctantly: "Yes, I agree."

"Now," I said, "let us look at this conception closely. According to you, god is a being than which nothing greater can be conceived. This being is defined and understood in terms of basic, derivative ideas such as wisdom, power, goodness, and absoluteness. For example, the idea of 'wisdom' implies reason and understanding, and the idea of 'creation' implies cosmic design and love. I mean to say that when we think of or conceive 'god,' we conceive the idea of an absolute being in the sense I have just explained. Would you agree?"

"Yes."

"Is this also what the faithful think of or conceive when they think of or conceive the being they worship? And is this the kind of being they worship on Sunday morning?"

"Yes—"

"Do they view themselves as worshipping a being other than this being when they worship god?"

"No, because they cannot, and because they would be worshipping an unknowable being."

"It should follow that the faithful do not worship god in himself—the true god—when they go to church to worship him. They worship an idea of a god that was first constructed by the founders of the church. Would you agree?"

"It seems that I have no choice."

"It should also follow that the idea of god they worship is a reflection or image of humanity, because the constitutive elements of this idea—beauty, goodness, wisdom, creativity, and their derivatives—are not only ideas constructed by the human mind but also ideals of human nature. Accordingly, the concept of god they worship is the concept of humanity *writ large, absolutely large*. It is an absolutization of the ideal that many human beings aspire to realize in their lives. Would you agree with this second inference?"

"I am not sure. But the Christian god is a responsive, caring god. He is a loving god."

"What if the faithful did not need him? Would they still worship him and pledge their devotion to him?"

My critic paused. She looked at me with thoughtful, curious eyes. "They would!" she said at last.

"Why?"

"Because he deserves reverence and devotion?" she said.

"Excellent answer!" I said.

"But the Christian god is a caring, responsive god. He would care for his people because he is caring."

"Is he? Has he ever responded to your prayers or paid attention to you when you were in trouble? In what way has he loved you or any other human being? Please, put aside the threats and promises concerning heaven and hell, because such promises are vacuous."

My critic looked at me with two dumbfounded eyes. "You must be a siren!" she mumbled.

"Well," I continued, "would you object if I said that the god that Christians worship is an idol—an idol constructed in the image of humanity?"

"An idol?" my critic cried impulsively, loudly. "This cannot be!"

"Why not?"

"Because they—we—believe that they worship the true god."

"But the true god surpasses their capacity of conception and comprehension and consequently of *believing*. Would you agree?"

My critic did not answer my question, so I pressed on. "Again, has anyone, even the founders of the church, personally encountered or tried to stand in the presence of god? If the answer to this question is 'no,' and it is 'no,' how can they pretend to worship him? How can they speak in his name or design a way to worship him if they never encounter him or make an attempt to feel his presence? The god they have offered to the people is, in fact, none other than Jesus! Is this why Jesus and his mother figure more prominently in the Bible and in liturgy than god? If the Christian conception of god is a substitute for the true god, is this another form of idolatry?"

"But Jesus is god and man in one nature—one being," she said. At this, I could not help but smile. My interlocutor noticed the smile, a clear indication of my disapproval. "The unity of god and man in Jesus," she added with emphasis, "is a *mystery!*"

"Is this idea another human construct, or perhaps a theological trick, from the founders of the church? Did they not convene and agree to add it as a means to consolidating the power of Constantinople and Antioch against Alexandria? I know this is a big theological issue. Please take what I have just said only as a hint."

"What you have just said is outrageous!"

"Maybe. Look at this mystery more realistically, more rationally, and more honestly. Who would have first pledged to Christianity if Jesus were simply a heroic, religious, or moral reformer? Or if he were simply one among many prophets? Without belief in Jesus the way *he was presented by his disciples and friends*, there would not be a basis for belief in immortality, last judgment, heaven, and hell. Would the clergy have any power or influence without these four ideas—or instruments of power? Hell is still used by many priests as a whip that keeps the faithful in line!

"You see," I continued, "no one of the disciples was a mystic, and no one understood the mystical and frequently metaphysical statements Jesus made about god. And yet, Jesus was the center of their attention and interest. He was their model of genuine prophecy, moral leadership, and advocacy for the sick, the poor, the disenfranchised, and the oppressed. Later on, the leaders who wrote Christian doctrine and method of worship did not have a mystical encounter with god; they did not even come close to the radiance of his presence, because no one of them made any reference to or betrayed any knowledge of such an encounter. In writing Christian doctrine, their eyes were on *Jesus, the son of god*—the god who is infinite in every possible mode of being and who defies any description or thought.

"Can you think, or imagine, this inconceivable relation—the infinite begetting a son? What kind of magician, what kind of mad person, what kind of sophist could foist such a travesty on the human mind? And yet, those founders foisted this and other travesties on the minds of their followers. What is strange is that they dubbed them 'mysteries' that no one could question or even discuss because they included them as elements of the revealed truth. You have to accept them on faith! I—"

"Are you trying to befuddle my mind? Yes, you must be a siren!" my critic suddenly intervened.

"Not at all! The question is whether the mind of the Christian worshipper is befuddled or whether it is silenced, sedated, or all three. I have no desire to participate in the thorny, muddled, and boring arguments, interpretations, explanations, and silly definitions of theologians. I am only trying, by means of rational conversation, to direct your attention to the logic and nature of the *basis of the Christian conception* of worship that has been overlooked by most, if not all, Christians.

"You see, the Christian leaders were not interested in the true god. In contrast, Jesus was a seeker of the true god. He, not they, lived according to the light of the truth that emanated from god. He was smitten by that light. How can you be afraid of ridicule, torture, or death after you are smitten by that light? I am convinced that Jesus derived his wisdom, his courage, his power to love, and his understanding of the meaning of human life from that light. For him, the natural domain is sacred; it is a direct emanation from god's being. This insight should, I think, be the basis of our respect not only for animals and plants but also for natural objects.

"What is uppermost on my mind is whether worshipping god should be restricted to one or two hours a week and whether or not Christians worship the true god. We might add a corollary to these two questions: does the Christian way of worshiping god provide an adequate experience of revering and praying to him, assuming that god needs this or a similar type of worship? I am inclined to think that human beings need to worship god, and that the details of the rituals they practice should arise not from god but from the beliefs, values, norms, customs, and traditions that the worshippers share as a community. I wonder whether you might be interested in this kind of conversation."

"Frankly, listening to your way of thinking, and especially to your way of looking at the basis of worshipping god, is provocative and at once disturbing. Nevertheless, I find it seductive. I would like to hear your view of these questions, but on one condition."

"What is it?"

"If you permit me to ask you questions and to disagree with you."

"Nothing pleases more than to receive questions and objections to my views."

"Excellent!"

"I have one more request," my critic said with a shy look on her face.

"Please, feel free to ask any question you may have!"

"It is getting a bit late. Can we resume our conversation tomorrow in this place at the same time?"

"Certainty!" I said. My critic vanished the instant I responded to her question.

How did this mysterious critic, this mysterious woman, this caring, empathic human being, know that I was tired? Why did she vanish suddenly without giving me a chance to thank her? Did she intentionally vanish this way? Is it because she did not want me to ask her questions about her identity? But she should know that any reasonable human being would be curious about her identity! *How* could she vanish this way? My puzzlement about her was slowly changing into apprehension. And yet, I decided to keep the stoic's attitude, for it had served me in our conversations this far.

Chapter Three

The Three Books of Knowledge

" **M** IGHT we begin our discussion of the questions I raised at the end of our last conversation?" my critic asked soon after she greeted me with a cheerful "good morning," not allowing me to digress into other kinds of question or points of interest. She was keen on keeping her identity in the dark.

"Of course!" I said with a smile on my lips. "If I am not mistaken, you are interested in knowing whether worshipping god should be restricted to a two-hour event once a week. Whether or not it is justifiable, and whether or not the Christian form or worship provides an adequate experience of revering and praying to god. Am I correct?"

"Yes, you are."

"To begin, we should recognize that worshipping god once a week in a building designated for this purpose is based on two basic assumptions: first, that god transcends, or exists outside of the universe he created. God is spiritual in nature, whereas the universe is material in nature. These two types of reality are generically different from each other. They do not mix. Second, that god is understood *anthropomorphically*—in human terms. As I explained earlier, in Christianity, god is understood as a human being writ 'absolutely large'. He thinks and acts the way human beings think and act, but he does so absolutely. For example, human beings create, love, feel, and punish; similarly, god creates, loves, feels, and punishes, but he does these things absolutely.

"In short, Christians view god as an absolute human being. Accordingly, because god is transcendent, a meeting place is needed. After all, he is the sort of being with whom one can have a personal relationship, and when people need help, especially in times of crisis, they feel justified in erecting a special building for revering and praying to him. But, are these two assumptions correct? Doubtful! What if god is not only transcendent but also immanent in the universe he created? What if he is not understandable or describable in human terms? Consequently, what if he neither needs worship nor asks to be worshipped? How should we understand or evaluate the phenomenon of worship, then? Would you agree to this way of formulating the question of worship?"

"Yes, only if it is considered in the context of the preceding discussion," my critic said.

"Of course."

"The concept of *immanence* that you discussed briefly earlier intrigues me," she said. "How can the infinite be immanent in the finite? More concretely, how can god, or the idea of god, than which nothing greater can be conceived, and which seems to resist our capacity of comprehension, be immanent in his creation? I understand the lexical meaning of 'immanent,' but I find it difficult to think about it at the existential or ontological level. Can you shed some light on this question?"

"I shall try."

"Very good. Trying is, most of the time, a forward step!"

"When I say that the infinite is immanent in the finite, I mean that it permeates it; it infuses its fabric, or it is present in it as a whole. I also mean that it shines through it. Consider for a moment the body of a human being. It is living in virtue of the fact that life permeates it. Life animates all of its cells. If, for some reason, life leaves any cell or organ, the cell or organ instantly dies; it ceases to be a living organism. Immanence is a state in which something is omnipresent in another object in the fulness of its being. This *something* acts on the object in which it is present and changes it in some way. In the case of plants and animals, the omnipresence of *life enlivens the plant*. The relationship between the two is causal. The first, life, acts on the material object and enables it to grow. Life is the *cause*, whereas growth, which is the essence of life, is the *effect*.

"When I say that the infinite is immanent in the universe, I mean that its being permeates the universe; it acts on it, and the outcome is its continual existence as a process. I also mean that the universe emanates from god the way light emanates from the sun, but with one major difference: god is infinite in its being. We can, metaphorically speaking, say that if our sun and the many other suns that dot the fabric of the universe, is the source of life and being on Earth, god is the sun of all suns. God acts on the universe and endows it not only with its existence, which is continual because the immanence is continual, but also with life, as in the realm of living things, and with consciousness, as in the realm of human beings. As an emanation from the infinite being of god, the universe reflects or reveals only one dimension of his being. We cannot explain or even understand how the universe exists or continues to exist if we do not grant that god is immanent in it. It is god's eternity that defies change and preserves the continual existence of the universe as process. Without this immanence, the universe collapses into nothing.

I continued. "But I am making a stronger claim: god did not merely create the universe the way a carpenter creates a chair or the way an artist creates an artwork. *The universe emanates from the depth of his being.* Here, the concept of *creation is replaced by the concept of emanation.* This emanation is astonishing in its diversity—matter, life, mind—because it shows that god is an inexhaustible wealth of being whose essence is an *infinite spring of creation.* Cast a quick, investigative, look at the human imagination. Is this power not a fountain of novel forms of being? Is it an accident that some metaphysicians defined the concept of god in terms of creativity? Although I cannot discuss it in any detail here, I can say to you with a reasonable measure of confidence that mind is the highest mode of cosmic creation—that it is closest to god and reveals his nature more than any other mode of creation does."

"Do you mean that nature in all its dimensions—plants, animals, and physical objects—is a part of god?"

"Yes, these dimensions emanate from his being the way light emanates from the sun."

"But—" my critic began but then paused. She looked at me with a pair of puzzled eyes. I understood the cause, so I went on.

"Do you think the claim that the universe is an emanation from god, and therefore, a part of it, is strange?" I asked.

"Yes, I do."

"Suppose we say that god created the universe, and suppose we hold that the universe exists separately from god. Where did the universe come from? You would say that god is the creator. Fine. But where did the stuff of the universe come from? Nothing? Notice: nothing must be something in order to be the source of this stuff. So, we can ask where did nothing come from? Again, *nothing* in the sense that total negation does not exist. If it did, god would not anymore be *than which nothing greater can be conceived.* You see, if god created the universe, he must be its source. The reason you resist the idea that nature emanates from and is a part of god is that the religious establishment, which is made up of an army of clerics and theologians, has foisted on the mind of the faithful the notion that god is pure spirit. But this is, I think, a prejudice that served society in the past but has lost its relevance in the present.

"By the way, why should you frown upon matter? Do you not enjoy the beauty of nature? Is nature not the source of your life? Do you not enjoy the feeling of life? Do you frown upon or hate your body? Do you not enjoy touching the body of your beloved? Do you not feel the warmth of her spiritual heart through her body? Again, is your body not the center from which your humanity emanates? When you are in the heat of the loving act, of listening to a beautiful piece of music, or when you are lost to a deep train of thought, are you aware of the distinction between your mind and body? Alas! Look at the sphere of nature: does the plant not derive its life from the soil? Do human beings not derive life from plants and animals?

"Why do we not instead say that whatever god created is good. God created nature, therefore nature is good. Who are we to decide what god should be? Can you, as a human being, not be spiritual? Does the fact that you have a body prevent you from being a spiritual being? Furthermore, if god is an infinite wealth of being, is it not possible that not only matter but also limitless types of realities emanate from him? Does this not reveal the infinite power, wisdom, and goodness of god?"

"I follow your line of reasoning," my critic said. "If god is immanent in the universe he created, if he does not exist outside it, then it would be practically impossible to anthropomorphize him, although we can talk about him metaphorically the way we are now doing. We can use human language as a ladder that leads us to a deeper understanding of his nature and closer to the infinity of his depth. The expressive function of language stops there."

"Your inference is, I think, correct," I said. "Now, let me ask whether you would agree that plants are superior *in their being*—not necessarily in their value—to rocks, water, or air because they are *living matter*?"

"I would."

"Would you also agree that dogs and monkeys are superior to physical objects and plants in that they possess consciousnesses, intelligence, and a measure of freedom?"

"I would."

"Would you also agree that human beings are superior to all the other types of reality in the universe because in addition to life, intelligence, and matter, they possess reason and the capacity of self-consciousness?"

"I follow your line of reasoning, and I doubt that anyone would reject it."

"Please, allow your mind to reflect on these levels of reality and view them as emanations from god—the way the rays that illuminate our Earth are emanations from our sun. In this request, I am asking you to begin this reflective process with an empirical observation of these different levels of reality, beginning from the lower to the higher, the way an airplane takes off the ground and flies into the sky. I want to make certain that this reflective process originates from and is tethered to the physical realm—that which is absolutely real and whose existence no one can doubt—"

"You are a meticulous and cautious thinker," my critic said, interrupting my train of thought.

I continued. "It is crucially important to emphasize that the ascent toward the infinite being of god is not an imaginary, arbitrary, or idiosyncratic activity or quest. Rather, it proceeds from the perception of a basic dimension of reality, which frequently begins with an encounter with an object in that dimension, and then, having penetrated *the fabric of its essence*, which is interconnected with the infinite web of reality, it gradually moves to the higher dimensions onward to the farthest possible horizon of human encounter."

"In the case of the sun," my critic interjected, "the eyes move upward toward it. In this case, it knows its destination; but what is the destination of the contemplative eyes that seek the source of the universe? Pardon me for the interruption."

"On the contrary, I should thank you for this extremely important question. You have been following the thread of my argument carefully."

My critic smiled.

I continued. "The first major stop on its way to its destination is the edge—""

"The edge?" the critic interrupted, this time with a frown on her forehead. "What edge?"

"The edge of the universe."

"But if the universe is an emanation from god, can there be an edge?"

"Yes, insofar as it is perceivable by the mind. The edge is that point, line, or horizon that distinguishes but does not separate the universe from what lies beyond it. It is the point beyond which the mind cannot conceive of anything?"

"What is the focus of this reflective process?"

"It is important to stress that this process is not a psychological or sensuous process in which the body moves from one point to another point in space and time. It is a purely *reflective process*. It is performed by the intellect. If you remove the intellect from it, the world around you darkens. The intellect is the faculty that enables us to see clearly, think clearly, imagine intuitively, and understand synoptically. In this process, the eye of the intellect should aim at the infinite, not as a concrete object but as the being that underlies the universe, as its source, as the power that animates it.

"Do we not frequently see the cause in the effect we experience, even though the cause is not directly given? Do we not feel love in an action performed by someone, even though love is not given as an object? The intellect can transcend the object of an experience to what causes, underlies, or is immanent within it. But in our pursuit of the infinite, we should keep a steady eye on a deeper mode of being. Not on what causes or underlies this or that object, but what causes or underlies the totality of being—the being from which everything emanates. This kind of perception is intuitive in character; it is the most fundamental cognitive activity the human mind can undertake. It is *pre-reflective*, and it is what gives rise to the different categories, concepts, notions, relations, images, symbols, interpretations, and every possible mode of cognition.

"Now I can respond to your question more directly. In our endeavor to move closer to the infinite, we should carefully read three books: the book of nature, the book of civilization, and the book of the human heart. Each one of these books is a source of a basic type of knowledge. These three types of knowledge constitute an amazing mosaic. Although they are read separately, they make up a harmonious whole, and I venture to say that they imply each other in the sense that no one can be adequately understood without reading and understanding the others. They are a harmonious whole because they are founded in and point to the infinite. We can say that they reveal three basic dimensions of our experience of the infinite.

"I have referred to these three sources of knowledge as "books," metaphorically of course, only to emphasize the need for reflection when we try to penetrate, by meditative activity, the fabric of these dimensions. Reflection, not argument, is the royal road that leads to the infinite, because our aim is not to persuade or demonstrate a certain proposition but to see, feel,

40

and understand the most fundamental mode of being. To be in the radiant presence of the being that underlies all being. This does not mean that this kind of reflection is not logical; on the contrary, logical thinking is one of its significant moments. In this activity, we do not merely consider the logical relationships between the premises of an argument but also the signification of these premises. It is *dialectical* in character; it endows knowledge in general and argument in particular with a life of its own. Without this life, thought remains impotent; with it, thought unites us with its object and transforms an idea of it into genuine belief. But, alas, genuine belief is the source of genuine faith!

"The book of nature is composed of two chapters. The first deals with nature as an order and as a cosmic process. We can read some of this book directly by confronting or experiencing it by means of the five senses. This experience reveals a spatial-temporal order and reveals what is generally known as a stellar system: land, water, sun, space, sky, mountains, air, planets, and the starry heaven beyond. This order is microscopically and macroscopically in motion. Although we do not usually reflect on this order—on its cause, nature, and purpose—because most of the time we are occupied with the enterprise of daily living, we can, and many of us do, take a break from our daily schedule to reflect on it.

"How did it come about? What power designed and weaved it? What underlies the appearance of the things we perceive with the five senses? Why did this power design this but not some other order? The more the human intellect probes these and related questions, the more it finds itself confronted with a mystery. Yes, mystery envelopes the order of nature, but it also permeates it. Human beings have been bewildered by this mystery ever since the fire of curiosity was kindled in the human mind about ten thousand years ago. I do not exaggerate in saying that the quest for the *arche*—that is, the stuff out of which nature is made—has been a permanent concern of human beings since the dawn of human civilization. If we view nature as a book, reading it should be the first step in our quest for the infinite."

"How does one read this book *reflectively*?" my critic asked.

"Reading it reflectively is a penetrative, analytic, and integrative activity. It aims at *seeing* the object in its internal and external relations. Internally, the mind seeks to grasp the nature of the elements that make up the object it is trying to understand in terms of the dynamics of their inter-relatedness, and comprehends them as a whole. Externally, it seeks to grasp the object in its complex inter-relatedness to the environment of which it is a part and tries to understand it in terms of and *as a part of* this relatedness."

"You seem to assume that the objects that make up the order of nature do not exist discretely but as parts of a larger whole," my critic said. "Am I correct?"

"Yes, and even the order of nature itself does not exist discretely or as an independent realty but as a part of a larger whole. Let me illustrate this point by an example. Focus your attention on this apple tree. At first, this tree seems to exist as an independent object, and in fact, we tend to interact with it as such. Do we not interact with cars, chairs, houses, tables, or computers as independent objects? But does this apple tree *actually* exist as an independent object? If we fix our attention reflectively on this tree, that is, on its parts internally and externally, we discover that the parts—trunk, bark, branches, leaves, fruits, sap, and roots, are essentially, indeed vitally, interconnected. The same applies to the other parts of its environment— soil, air, light, water, gravity.

"In fact, a critical examination of their relatedness will show that the object derives its being and its functions as the tree it is, made from these parts, which also exist as organically interrelated components within a wider environment. There are no gaps in the scheme of nature. It is internally and externally *plentiful*—a *chain of being*. The experience of any object, and here I mean comprehending it in its internal and external relatedness, always takes place in terms of its proximate and larger environments. Whether I reflectively confront this tree, the sun, the grain of sand, the waft of air that now glides over my face, or the sensation of hunger I am now experiencing, I assure you that the process of reflection will ceaselessly proceed, internally and externally—some would say to infinity. Could it be that this kind of reflection justifies the mind in its quest for the cause and nature of this amazing universe? But if the universe, the way it is given to our senses, is a *plenum,* can we locate its cause outside it?"

"Your argument seems to lead to the conclusion that god does not transcend the universe in the sense of existing outside it," my critic said, "but is immanent in it. Am I correct?"

"Your inference is correct. By the way, let us grant, for the sake of discussion, that god ontologically transcends the universe. How can the mind know that it exists? Please, do not bring in the idea of faith, which is a big concoction of the early founders of the church and a sad travesty on reason, because faith can neither argue nor introduce anything. Faith is made of *petrified belief* without awareness of its source or whether it is true or false, justified or justifiable. A faithful person may be willing to learn about matter, art, or life—or even about other religions that she treats as cultural phenomena—but not about her religious beliefs. This is primarily because she *feels convinced*, without knowing how or why, that these are indubitably true. She has grown up with them the way she has grown up with ears, legs, and speaking a certain language.

"Accordingly, I shall not bring in the idea of faith but the idea of *causation*, according to which nothing exists or happens in the universe without a cause. Regardless of how the effect is produced, and regardless of the kind of relation it has to the cause, in the sense of creation, the effect always, in some way, reflects the nature of the cause, mainly because it comes from it. Thus, regardless of whether god, as a cause, is immanent or transcendent, the universe reflects some basic features of the nature of god. These features can be a basis for constructing a concept of god."

"This line of reasoning is, I think, valid, but the urgent question that demands an answer is that if god is transcendent, how do we know that the universe he created reflects features we can attribute to him? If we cannot experience him directly, it would be very difficult to verify any knowledge we claim of him. When we say that god transcends the human mind, because he cannot be an object of knowledge, we, by this very fact, undercut the possibility of attributing any kind of knowledge to him, even knowledge of his existence. But on the other hand, if we say that god is immanent in the universe, we can *also* say that he is transcendent, only in the sense that although we cannot experience his presence or radiance, we cannot know him in himself."

"What you say is interesting," my critic said. "I find it intellectually seductive, but I cannot give my full assent to it. I need to think for some time about the implications of your view."

"I understand your hesitation. It is not a widely held view. But I shall be happy to discuss it with you at a time of your choice."

"Good."

"I can now proceed to the second chapter of the book of nature. This chapter is written by empirical scientists. Naked, by their efforts alone, the senses cannot know the essence or inner nature of the universe. They can, in principle, know the appearance of things but not the way they are within themselves. The mystery that provokes the mind to inquire into the cause, nature, and purpose of the universe deepens and expands in its scope when we wonder about the essence of the phenomena that constitute the

43

structure of the universe. What power, or *daemon*, thinks, feels, and wills in me, a human being? What makes the tree or the horse grow? What is the stuff that constitutes the *being* of things?

"The answer to these and many related questions that were first posed by philosophers in the early period of ancient Greece's golden age and continue to be pondered by natural scientists today have reached a high point of progress in the twenty-first century. Although our knowledge of matter, life, and human nature is highly refined and deserves the utmost respect and admiration, modern science has not yet lifted the veil of mystery that envelopes and penetrates the universe. What if someone were to reflect on the detailed accounts of a physicist, chemist, biologist, geologist, and cosmologist and weave these accounts into a *conceptual image* the way an artist weaves sounds into a symphony or words into a novel. Can you imagine the amazing richness of this image? Next, what if someone weaves an image based on her sensuous perceptions of the universe as an ordered whole the way contemporary cosmologists try to do? Let us weave out of these two images a third image that reveals the structure of the world in its internal and external dimensions. Yes, what if she reflects on this marvelous work that is an intellectual narrative of the universe and that will, by necessity, be a lengthy, reflective, and patient process?

"Let me at once emphasize that this reflective reading is tantamount to an analytical, exploratory, and integrative activity; it begins with reading a particular object as a center and advances from this epicenter to the periphery of the universe, toward the farthest perceivable horizon the human mind can reach. I say 'can' because the human mind cannot, as I mentioned earlier, comprehend the total realm of reality but only an emanation of it. And as an emanation, it is finite. The more we advance in our reflection on the inner and outer structures of the universe, the closer we move toward the edge.

"The second book the intellect should read in its endeavor to move closer to the edge is the book of the history of human civilization. By 'human civilization,' I mean the major accomplishments of human beings throughout the world in the areas of art, philosophy, religion, science, politics, technology, morals, and ways of achieving happiness in the course of history. This history is the history of the *human spirit* in its effort to realize the potentialities that constitute the structure of the human essence. These potentialities are the sparks that inspired and continue to inspire the artist in her quest for beauty, the philosopher in her quest for the nature of values, the scientist in her quest for knowledge, the social reformer in her quest for justice and freedom, and the ordinary person in her quest for happiness.

"The human spirit dwells in its accomplishments the way an artist dwells in her art, and the way human beings dwell in their actions. We know the character of an individual by a thoughtful examination of her accomplishments, not by what she says or feels about herself. Do we not feel the artist's soul reverberating in her work? Do we not know the kind of artist she is? Do we not evaluate her contributions to society in and through this examination? Again, do we not feel the pulse of the human spirit in the accomplishments of Eastern, Middle Eastern, African, and Western civilizations? Alas! Does this pulse not originate from the same source—human nature? Do we not feel the fire of human passion for love, beauty, god, happiness, knowledge, immortality, and survival emanating from these accomplishments?

"It is, I think, reasonable to say that the history of civilization is the ultimate source of our knowledge of human nature—some would say the only source. We know what it means to be a human being by a careful study of history—of the monumental works human beings left in science, religion, government, humanities, and ways of realizing happiness. This study should disclose what human beings *can and should* do, both individually and collectively. This claim is based on the firm assumption that human nature is a *dynamis*, or a power. As such, it can be used for both constructive and destructive purposes."

"But you seem to emphasize the constructive power—why?" she asked.

"I cannot deny that war and destruction are some of the most notable legacies of humanity, and that the lives of ordinary people in every society and historical period were vitiated with hate, oppression, injustice, exploitation, and ignorance. But who said that the wheels of rational, moral, and cultural progress grind fast in the course of time? Should we not recognize that human nature is a bundle of potentialities, and that human progress is always a goal, always a challenge? I agree with you that we should not ignore or underestimate the dark, destructive side of human beings in the past, the present, and certainly in the future.

"In this context, I emphasize the constructive power of human nature, because broadly speaking, the constructive purposes figure more prominently in the course of history. Can you imagine what our world would be like today if the dark side of human nature had prevailed over the constructive one? Would we be having this rational conversation now—or the present explosion in science, technology, art, philosopher, and moral progress—without the prevalence the constructive side of human nature?"

"Can you shed some light on the claim that history is the ultimate source of our knowledge of human nature?"

"Gladly!" I chimed. "Let us imagine a magician—one who brings things and events into being and makes them vanish by some kind of incantation or wand. You must have seen these magicians when you were a teenager."

"Yes, I did."

"Now, imagine a magician who can *actually* make the history of human civilization vanish from existence. Suppose such magician actually wiped out the history of the human race so that no libraries, art, science, religion, social institutions, languages, computers, cities, or monuments— in short, no trace of human accomplishments or existence—remains, not even what happened a few hours ago. Let us also imagine that all older people were struck with a sudden case of amnesia and so cannot remember anything about the past. What would the world look like?"

"Like the world in the Stone Age."

"Why?"

"Because without the knowledge that has been accumulating over the past centuries in books, knowledge banks, oral memory, and social institutions, we cannot have technology, art, science, religion, or anything that is often considered an element of civilized existence."

"But although the people who populated that age were primitive, they were human; they possessed the capacity to evolve at the human level. Would you agree?

"Yes."

"What makes them human? They, in some way, possess the *human essence*. This essence existed in them as a potentiality that was not yet realized. If it did not exist, the human species would not have developed any kind of civilized behavior. I submit the hypothesis that the history of civilization is *the history of the continual realization of the potentialities that make up the structure of human nature: the powers of thinking, feeling, and willing.* The first aims at knowledge, and its highest value is wisdom; the second aims at love and beauty, and its highest value is happiness; and the third aims at freedom, and its highest value is goodness. The more our intellect probes reflectively the nature of these values and their derivatives in the multitude of human accomplishments, the more we grow in our understanding of the realm of humanity.

"But in contrast to the realm of nature, which is given by a power superior to us, this realm is *extra-natural* and cannot be understood in natural terms, primarily because it is a creation of the human mind, which also cannot be understood in natural terms. As you can see, human beings live in two realms. They live in nature through their bodies and they live in the realm of humanity through their minds. But the world they create is multidimensional. It is a world of ideas—theories, visions, images, laws, values, and a world of practice—action, life, technology, institutions, and policies. What are accomplishments in physics, chemistry, geology, technology, art, religion, philosophy, and government—in short, the materially and culturally built environment—but creations of the human mind? The map of this world is rather large and complex. It originated from the human mind, and it discloses the remarkable ingenuity, intricacy, mystery, and greatness of human nature.

"Do we not see humanity present when we examine a machine—a bridge, a ship, an airplane? When we read the different philosophical systems that punctuate the history of civilization? When we experience the music, paintings, dance, dramas, literature, sculpture, and photography of the different cultures of the world? When we contemplate the worldviews of the different religions? And when we stand before the ruins of ancient civilizations in the East and the West? Do such works not speak to us, revealing the marvelous dynamics, story, and aspirations of our humanity?"

"But they belong to the past, and the past does not exist!" my critic said.

"The past does not exist, and the human beings who made it do not exist. But let me remind you that the past exists in us—in you, me, the artist, the scientist, the social reformer, the teacher, the farmer, the engineer, and every civilized human being who thrives on the face of the Earth. Is it an accident that people in the past and the present honor their past leaders, scientists, philosophers, theologians, artists, and soldiers? Again, as I mentioned a moment ago, would we be having this conversation? Would the different societies of the world be pursuing their life-projects if the cultural legacies of the past did not exist? The cultural achievements of the past comprise *the creative heart* that beats in the present. They are the well from which we receive our inspiration and the stuff of any future accomplishment."

"I now have a clearer understanding of what you mean when you speak of a human realm that exists side by side to the natural realm," my critic said. "But I do not yet have a clear idea of how a reflective contemplation of this realm can move us closer to the edge."

"Has it occurred to you that the realm of human accomplishments is as complex, as vast, as mysterious, as rich, and I think richer than the realm of nature is?"

"Richer?"

"Yes, richer!" I exclaimed.

"Can you explain how it is richer?"

"The realm of nature *is given*. It evolves, but its evolution is governed by laws. It is a realm of necessity, not of freedom. The stone acts as a stone and cannot be other than what it is unless certain natural conditions prevail, which are also governed by natural laws, or unless a person transforms it into a statue or a building block. But the human realm is a realm of realized value; every human institution, organization, action, and establishment is the outcome of a design; every design is a response to a purpose; every purpose expresses a type of value; and every realized value is a moment of growth and development for human nature. For example, science exists as a response to the need for knowledge, the army exists as a response to the need of defense, art exists as a response to the need of beauty, and so on. By its very essence value exists as a potentiality for infinite realization. Whether it is art, education, business, farming, or any other activity we perform in the different areas of our life, the *possibilities of creation are limitless*.

"The more we grow in our understanding of human nature, the more we discover new ways of realizing them. Compare the human world today to that of the middle ages or to the world of the ancient Greeks and Romans? What are the major differences between them? What are the differences in the magnitude of realized value? What if the intellect reflectively penetrates the realm of human accomplishments? Do you not think that our intellect would begin with an object, regardless of whether it was simple or complex, in one area of accomplishment, which would form a kind of epicenter and then gradually move outward to the periphery? Would it not move from one dimension to another in that all human values are organically inter-related, and continues to move toward the periphery until it reaches the edge?"

"And the edge is—?" my critic snapped.

"The edge of the human realm."

"I have a feeling that what you say is reminiscent of that famous line from Shakespeare—'to be or not to be.'"

"To some extent, Hamlet stood at the edge of the realm of his being. What did it mean for him, and for any other human being, 'to be or not to be' in that particular situation? Could he *be* in the real sense of *being* if he were not true to himself as a human being? By standing on that edge, he bordered the depth of the infinite."

"But how does the human realm border this depth and be simultaneously extensive with it, given that it is an emanation of it?"

"We discern the border when our reflective intellect moves from the epicenter to the periphery of the realm of human accomplishments, that is, after it grasps the richness of their being and meaning, which is no mean task! In this process it does not only stand at the edge of its own being but also at the edge of the human realm as such."

"Although you use them metaphorically, the ideas of the books of nature and human accomplishments are not, *qua* ideas, foreign to my way of thinking. But the idea of the human heart is, to confess, foreign to me and I think to many people."

"This confession does not surprise me. Philosophers and ordinary people have, for centuries, viewed the rational faculty as distinct and independent of the affective faculty and have frequently viewed the two concepts as antagonists. But this view, to my mind, is mistaken. I am inclined to think that both originate from a single source. This source is what I call the *human heart*. Any rational action we undertake is permeated by emotional content, and every emotional activity we undertake is permeated by rational content. Do we not *feel* the meaning of our ideas, and do we not see the truth of our emotions, at least sometimes? Do social scientists these days not speak of *emotional intelligence*? Do we not *feel* that we should act this or that way or make this or that choice? Many people think that ideas are abstract, cold-blooded entities. But are they? How can the mind think about abstract entities? Mind is life. What it thinks is dynamic and living. Otherwise, it cannot think it. It is more reasonable to say that an idea is a drop of meaning, and as such, that it is a drop of life.

"But how can it be such a drop if it is not animated by passion, by emotion? Suppose you voluntarily or involuntarily think an idea the way we are doing at this moment. Thinking cannot be reified. Otherwise, it is not thinking. It is an event, and events cannot be reified. But thinking is not a material but a human event; it does not issue from a mind as an immaterial entity existing independently, and it does not function according to peculiar laws apart from the other faculties that make up the structure of human individuality but from the individual as a subject, as a multidimensional being, and as the unity of these dimensions. The 'I' that thinks in me feels what it thinks, and the 'I' that feels an emotion in me thinks what it feels."

"Does this mean that these two functions blend or collapse into each other?"

"No, it only means, like I have just indicated, that intelligence permeates emotional activity, and that emotions permeate rational activity. They are androgynous. They have this dual nature not only because they originate from the same source but also because they are nourished by it. Now, I can say that *the human heart* is the most astonishing, most mysterious reality we encounter in the fabric of human nature. It is impossible to call someone human if she does not think, feel, and will. Do we not exonerate a child or a mentally sick person from moral and legal responsibility simply because they cannot make rational decisions, control their emotions, and will their actions? But these three faculties do not function apart from each other; they are interdependent in their functions and modes of existence. What is the source, or basis, of their unity? What makes their interdependence possible? Regardless of whether we say that mind is a function of the brain or that it is an immaterial reality, these questions merit our special attention because the existence of the capacities that make up the structure of human nature are incontrovertible facts: they are the substance and foundation of our lives as human beings."

"Moreover, we do not need to subscribe to any theory of mind or to advance one in order to answer these questions. On the contrary, our answer should be based on the functions these capacities perform—that is, on what they do in our theoretical and practical lives. Can we not phenomenologically extrapolate the essence of these activities? Like the artist who reveals herself in her work or the human being who reveals herself in her action, can we not discern the dynamics of the human heart by an examination of what it does? Furthermore, do we need a theory of mind in order to examine what it actually does? What is the 'I' that acts as the subject and presides over its thinking, feeling, and willing activities? How does it perform the activity of self-consciousness? Delete the phenomenon of self-consciousness and you delete the whole phenomenon of humanity. Can we perform any activity, consciously and voluntarily, if we do not imply a self-conscious 'I' that is the author of the activity? But again, what is the power that engages us in the experience of self-consciousness? How can the self, which is a subject, be an object to itself but remain the subject that authors this act of self-consciousness? Or, how can the subject *recoil* upon itself, face itself, and be an object to itself at the same time?"

"What is more interesting is that this very self-consciousness is intimately connected with the question of personal identity: how do I know that I am the same person during any stretch of time, a moment or years ago, without knowing, without a shred of doubt, that I and everything that exists in this universe is constantly changing?"

"Memory!" my critic suddenly interjected.

"This is the traditional answer to the question of personal identity. I am afraid that many thinkers in the social sciences and the humanities still hold on to this explanation, but is it an adequate answer?"

"Is there a better answer?"

"We might not be able to advance a better answer, but we should first know why it is inadequate. What do you think?"

"What you say is logical."

"Let us grant, for the sake of discussion, that memory is the basis of personal identity: I know I am the same person I was moment ago because I remember that I am the same person. Consequently, when I undertake an activity of thinking, for example, of making a judgment, I know that the judgment comes from my mind. I know that I have made it because I remember that I am the same person who made it a moment ago, because I remember the process involved in making the judgment.

"But memory is not the subject that made the judgment nor the subject that remembered it. Memory cannot initiate action voluntarily. It is a mental event, an effect a subject remembers; as such, it is a necessary consequence of other events. I know that I was the same person I was a moment ago because I remember this event or fact. But who undergoes the act of thinking or of remembering, and who determines that I am the same person who performed the act of thinking? As you see, the concept of memory implies a subject that remembers. My main concern in this conversation is the *identity of this subject*.

"What is this subject? In raising this question, I am asking you to direct your attention to the source of the activities of thinking, feeling, and willing. Let me at once state that this subject cannot be a mental reality, for example, an immaterial entity, because it is the source of every mental event. Try to capture this entity in one mental grasp. No matter how much you try, you will never capture such an entity. But if you reflect on it, through different types of thinking, feeling, and willing that it performs, you will stand before a mystery. Not merely the kind that defies description or explanation but the kind that stands before you as a sun, as a luminous source, as the power that makes the activities of these capacities possible, and by inference, as the power that makes science, art, philosophy, and practical activity possible.

"The accomplishments of these capacities can be viewed metaphorically as rays emanating from *this luminous source*. This source sits at the base of everything we do as individuals, communities, and races. It is the source of self-consciousness and personal identity, and it is also the basis of our humanity. Perhaps you can now see why I characterized it as a sun. Everything spiritual in our lives originates from this sun. It is a flame of *spiritual fire*. The world of this flame is the world of the human heart. I call it the 'human heart' because it is the source of our humanity—of the capacities of thinking, feeling, and willing. We would make a grave mistake, as I pointed out earlier, if we viewed these capacities as being independent of each other. They derive their substance, their unity, and their life from this fire.

"Reflection on this spark in light of its accomplishments, on its essence as a source, and on the mystery that oozes out of its very being will lead the eyes of the reflective intellect away from the universe as a composite of individual objects and events to its farthest horizon. Now, let us ask this reflective intellect to dwell in its reflection on this luminous flame and let us ask it to grasp, so far as it can, the source of its being, its light, and its purpose. *How far* can it go in its reflection? We should never lose sight of the fact that it and the sun on which it reflects are finite—"

"It cannot go farther than the edge it has reached in its endeavor to grasp the being of the universe," my critic said.

"Yes, but with a difference."

"What is it?" my critic asked with open eyes.

"The mystery that oozes out of the luminous flame surpasses in its profundity, grandeur, and loftiness the mystery that envelopes the domain of the universe because it is exquisitely luminous and especially because it is *a source—a subject*! The reflective intellect moves toward the edge on the wings this mystery. What if the reflective intellect reads the three books of knowledge, that is, what if it contemplates the book of nature, of the history of civilization, and of the human heart? What if it contemplates the intricate web of their details—that is, of the dimensions of the world in which human beings thrive. Next, what if it moves in this process from its point of departure outward through every conceivable horizon to the farthest possible horizon. What if it stands at a horizon beyond which it cannot move. Yes, what if it stands at that edge—what then? What does it see? What can it see? Well, it might not be able to see clearly, and it might not be able to see at all because there are no objects it can see. But do you think that it will confront nothing? Of course, because the universe cannot rest on nothing. It must rest on being—something that exists—and that something must be superior to it. But what kind of being does it confront?"

"Have you stood on that edge?" my critic interrupted rather impulsively.

"On that edge?" I returned the question with a smile. "You have to read the three books I described, of course briefly, if you desire an answer to your question. But I think that the realm that overlooks that edge is quite different than the realm of nature because it surpasses, in its radiance, every imaginable type of reality. And yet, this realm, which is more real than the reality of the universe is, is an infinite realm of being. The reflective intellect experiences it as a source, as a sun, as a fountain, but it also experiences it as much more, infinitely much more.

"And when I say 'source,' I do not mean the kind of source we experience in nature or human life, for example, a spring as a source of water or mind as a source of ideas, but as *the source*, the source that transcends every conceivable source. I mean the source from which the *infinite forms* of being flow, the source from which truth, goodness, and beauty flow. The source that makes them shine with absolute importance and dignity. Although I am trying to describe it metaphorically, this source is indescribable, not only because it cannot, on principle, be described, but because the reflective intellect does not possess the conceptual categories by which it can describe it. It can see its radiance and understand it without really seeing or undersetting it. How can it describe it if it cannot comprehend it? And yet, it can see and understand this radiance!"

"What does it see? It cannot simply see blank or pure radiance. Therefore, it must see something else."

"What does it see?" I asked the same question rhetorically, impatiently.

"I mean the source. Does it see it as a source and know it as the source?"

"The source?" I asked rhetorically.

"Yes!" my critic answered with an air of embarrassment.

I almost told her yes, that all it can do in this event is stand in *reverent silence*, but I did not. Instead, I went on. "How can the reflective intellect truly see or understand when it stands before the radiance that dazzles its vision of the infinite depth of that radiance? In himself, god is transcendent. We can say that he is an infinite depth only because nature and the human mind are effluences from this depth, and because these emanations are continuous *with it and point to it*. But when the reflective intellect reaches the edge, it does not reach a line or a ledge the way we experience these things in nature and human life. Rather, it reaches the edge the way we experience the radiance of our sun when we stand in its light. And just as the sun is beyond the reach of our vision, the infinite depth of god is beyond the reach of our vision. Standing on the edge is, in fact, standing in god's radiance— in his presence. She who stands before this most dazzling spectacle, who is baptized by its light, who sucks the milk of her life from its breast, *lives from this light*. Please tell me, does a person who loves from and in this light need to go to church in order to worship a god she does not know?"

"On more than one occasion during your answers to my questions," my critic said, "I thought you were a magician, because you have a way of making your listener understand and believe what you say. You even made me feel that I was moving with you toward the edge where you must have stood. Otherwise, how can you chart the way that leads to it? I know you are reluctant to say whether you stood at that edge, but let me confess that your account is not only provocative but also enticing. You remind me of what my grandmother frequently said to me when I was a young woman: 'be ready for the truth when you stumble on it or when it surprises you. It has a charm of its own. Once it smites, it carves a place for itself on the wall of your mind.'"

"Your grandmother was a wise woman."

"I sometimes think that wisdom is frequently wasted on young people."

"Are you sure?"

"Maybe not, but I would like to continue our conversation tomorrow, if possible. However, I wonder whether you might answer a question that has been nagging my mind throughout this conversation."

"I shall always try."

"Thank you! How can an experience of the fluteplayer's music be a vehicle that transports us to the edge?"

"As art, the aesthetic object is a depth of meaning. The magnitude of this depth differs from one work to another. Some are superficial while others are rich. But in general, a work or art is great inasmuch as it is capable of creating a *profound* human experience—that is, of realizing a depth of meaning and revealing the truth of a dimension of the *nature of human life in a beautiful form.* The greater this depth, the closer we move toward the edge. But this movement is not a kind of jumping-off point, and it does not befall the aesthetic listener. Rather, it emerges from an already existing wealth of insight, knowledge, understanding physical reality, civilization, and human nature. For example, some people might read Dostoevsky's *The Brothers Karamazov* and Tolstoy's *The Death of Ivan Ilych* and find them boring wastes of time. But others might find them meaningful and discover new depths of meaning as they forge their way into maturity. The capacity to intuit any depth of meaning in any human creation in any area of inquiry reflects the depth of the mind that intuits them. The greater this depth, the greater its capacity to apprehend the meaning potential in the work.

"Not every person who listened to the music of the fluteplayer enjoyed or was touched by it, just like not everyone who listens to Bach's music enjoys it or feels touched by it. But let me assure you that the music of that fluteplayer was *exceptionally profound.* It was a vehicle that transports any seeker of meaning to the edge, primarily because it did not merely speak to the mind, merely to the affective faculty, or merely to the sensuous faculty but also to the human heart in the medium of its grasp of the three books I have discussed with you."

"I see," my critic said with thoughtful eyes. Then, and to my surprise, she abandoned me to a long gaze during which her eyes were not focused on me or on anything around me but on a small magnolia tree that stood high next to the rotunda. "You know," she said after she emerged from her daze, "people get intoxicated when they consume large quantities of alcohol or drugs, but I feel intoxicated when I participate in a meaningful conversation, regardless of whether it is in the form of monologue or dialogue. And let me admit to you that the question of the existence of god and the conditions under which we can have an audience with him, or at least feel his presence, makes me extremely intoxicated. I am a *god-intoxicated woman!* God is my ultimate passion. Our conversation has inflamed the fire of my desire to contemplate the road that leads to him that you have outlined poetically. Can we meet again tomorrow?"

"Of course!"

"I assure that I shall return to you with a load of questions."

A smile flitted on my lips. My critic did not speak with her lips but with her eyes. I understood the language she spoke. Sometimes, the language of silence speaks more lucidly than the language of the scientist or the philosopher does, even of the poet! Like she did in our previous encounters, my critic vanished from my presence without allowing me to say a word about anything. I remained seated on my bench, enfolded with puzzlement for several minutes, not knowing what to think or how to explain the miraculous presence of this critic, of this angel, of this supernatural human being.

Was she a human being? How can a human being appear and disappear from existence? How can such a being be a 'god-intoxicated woman?' Frankly, not only my mind but also my heart was beating fast when I was reflecting on this this phenomenon! It was impossible for me to explain or understand by logical means. I was only hoping that I would discover the truth sooner if not later. Patience was needed. Fortunately, I was a patient man.

Chapter Four

How I met the Fluteplayer

THE critic, who was at first my gadfly and gradually transformed my train of thought into a real conversation by becoming a real, an active interlocutor in it, now revealed her true identity—she was a seeker of god. Her appearance in my consciousness as an imaginary, hypothetical human being remains a mystery to me: how could she intrude into my consciousness if she were not an angel, as I had thought she was? Was she the *daemon* that had always lurked on the rim of my mind, always smiling when I thought or did something right or good, always frowning when I thought or did something wrong or bad? Was this *daemon* a reflection of my inmost self, of my inmost desire to be authentic? Suppose she was my *daemon*, or even my angel; how was she transfigured into a real human being? The mere thought of this question made my mind rock with fear. Alas, was she real? Was I hallucinating? Were all our conversations hallucinations? I know that sometimes some people hallucinate such encounters. Could it be that not only our past conversations were hallucinations but also all of our prospective conversation?

These questions occupied my attention when I was driving my car to Liberty Garden the following morning. Although I parked the car on the southern side of the parking lot, as I always did, I did not get out. I felt a strong, overwhelming desire to be certain of the real identity of this woman—whether she was a *daemon*, an angel, or a real human being. I felt powerless before this desire. Who was she? My interest in this question was gradually becoming an obsession. At the conclusion of our last conversation, she declared that she was a god-intoxicated woman. Fine! Where did she come from? How did she glide into my consciousness as an imaginary being and then into my life as a real person? She must be real, otherwise, all my conversations with her, including the ruminations I had about them, would be nothing but a series of phantasmagorias. But they are not—*cannot be* phantasmagorias. For some strange reason, her declaration that she was a god-intoxicated woman lingered in my mind more than any other question, fear, or anxiety.

What does it mean to be a god-intoxicated person? I had never met such a person before. Have you met such a person, dear reader? Would such a person live in a constant state of intoxication with god? Suppose she did, how would she feel and think? I have a hunch that she would think and live from the standpoint of god the way an alcohol-intoxicated person would think and live from the standpoint of alcohol. But what if a person is truly intoxicated with god? What if every fiber of her being was filled with god's presence, not with alcohol, would *she be real the way ordinary people are real?*

I do not remember how long I remained in my car, but I remember thinking about the implications of the idea of god-intoxication as I walked toward the rotunda. It is one thing for an alcoholic to act and think on the basis of how alcohol affects the nervous system, in which she is not in control of her thoughts, desires, or will. But it is something else for the god-intoxicated person to act on the basis of the divine presence in her mind and heart.

"Good morning!" my critic said with the most cheerful tone in her voice, interrupting my train of thought.

Somewhat timidly, I ascended the steps of the rotunda and extended a similar greeting to her. "Cheerful!" I noticed myself saying in a whispering voice.

"Why not?" the same whispering voice replied. "She is as real as you are, as the rotunda is, as the garden is, and as the sun that illuminates the Earth is.

"Are you sure?" the same voice whispered.

"Yes!"

"Then act accordingly" the voice said.

"But—" I could not respond to this last retort because my critic moved closer toward me and welcomed me to her presence. Frankly, I was overwhelmed by the warmth of her welcome. I responded to her with equal warmth. How could I, or any rational being, have acted differently? The woman who sat at the bench opposite me was not only real to my eyes and ears but an effulgence of *human presence.* The storm of questions, ideas, and anxieties that haunted me as I was driving my car to the garden receded into the back of my mind but did not leave entirely. Storms like this one do not die easily, and if they leave us, they do so reluctantly. Time is their judge and executor.

My critic began right away. "Your description of the fluteplayer and his music intrigued me; it generated in my mind a bundle of questions. All of them center on god, on his relationship to humanity, and especially on the conditions under which it is possible to be baptized by the radiance of his presence. I wonder whether I can ask you some of these questions." She looked at me inquisitively.

"Gladly," I said, "but on one condition."

"What is it?"

"I am neither an expert on god nor a mystic who has been smitten by god's radiant light, although I aspire to stand in that light. I shall do my best, but I cannot promise much."

"All I wish is to hear your views on god and the path that leads to him. But, before we begin our conversation, can I ask you for a small favor?"

I was startled by this request. "Favor?" I thought. "How can she ask for a favor if I do not even know her? Does she know me?" The question of her identity suddenly surged into my mind. "Should I ask her about her identity? Does she have an ulterior motive?"

These questions did not wait for answers, because the imperceptible smile with which she expressed her request was so charming that I could not resist it. "Of course!" I said involuntarily, as if my answer sprang from that charming smile.

"Did you personally meet the fluteplayer? Did you visit him? What kind of life did he lead?"

The doubts and fears that had found their way into my mind a moment ago vanished swiftly when I heard her question. Its impact was balsamic! "No," I said, "I did not meet him or speak with him personally. But I can say that I had an encounter with him."

"How can you have an encounter with a person you have not met?"

"My encounter with him was indirect."

"Indirect? You seem to speak in riddles. Can you explain this riddle?"

"I shall do my best. Broadly speaking, the defining feature of an encounter is not the mere fact of a physical encounter between two people but the active, productive interaction between them. This type of interaction is essentially intellectual, psychological, or spiritual in character. Do we not interact with people such as Plato, Newton, or Shakespeare when we read their works seriously, and do we not encounter Rembrandt, Michael Angelo, or Cezanne when we have a genuine aesthetic experience of their works? Do these thinkers and artists not dwell in their works?"

"How?"

"The artwork reflects the artist's worldview—that is, her basic beliefs and values, her understanding of the world, and the meaning and destiny of human life. Do we not visit Dostoevsky's tortured soul or Hesse's mystical soul when we read their works? Do we not, in general, visit the soul of the genuine writers and artists when we seriously visit their works? Do we not have *an encounter* with them when we have this kind of visit?"

"But the artists and thinkers you have mentioned are dead. How can one have an encounter with a dead person?"

"*Are* these thinkers and artists dead? First, what is a human being apart from her works or deeds? At the existential level, she is an abstraction outside of the domain of her works, regardless of whether this domain is small, large, rich, poor, or bad. Second, *are* the thinkers and artists I mentioned dead? Do they not live in their works the way you and I *now* live in ours? Can you know who I am except in and through my works? If you delete my actions or works, you delete me from the face of the Earth!"

"I understand the sense in which we can have an indirect encounter with an artist, philosopher, or scientist, but in what sense can we say that you had an indirect encounter with the fluteplayer?"

"My answer will be a little lengthy."

"Take your time, please! Frankly, I have never met or even heard of such a man as this fluteplayer. Your description of his music piqued my interest in him."

"Well, I moved to Jackson from Olive Branch, Mississippi, one year ago. The first thing I did when I settled in my apartment was to call Father Demetrius, pastor of St. John the Divine cathedral. I expressed my desire to join his church. He asked whether I was baptized as an Eastern Orthodox.

'Yes,' I said. 'I shall be happy to see you in my office,' he said.

"We arranged a meeting. The visit was cordial. He inquired about my religious background, my profession, and my family life. Then he asked me questions about life in general, and especially about the role of philosophy in human life. Having noticed that I had an accent, he inquired, 'Where were you born?'

'Antioch—' I said.

'California?' he inquired.

'No.'

'Where?'

'Turkey,' I said.

Father Demetrius's eyes glittered with curiosity. 'The original Antioch?'

'Yes,' I said.

He nodded his head approvingly. 'Then you are a Roman Orthodox.'

'Yes.'

'You are welcome to our church,' he said.

"This response confused me. Instead of feeling pleased that he had welcomed me to his church, I felt vexed and disappointed, because it became clear to me that joining his church entailed meeting certain formal conditions, as if the doors of his church should not, or could not, be open to anyone who did not meet those conditions, as if those conditions defined the meaning of 'Christian' or 'religiosity.' It is strange how many churches these days, contrary to the way it used to be, are more like social clubs that function according to certain rules, beliefs, rituals, norms, practices, and symbols without regard to the inner soul of the real person who thrives behind them.

"Somewhat reluctantly, I decided to join St. John the Divine cathedral. Even though I attended liturgy, which was elaborate and aesthetically impressive, I did not feel that I was standing in the presence of god during that ceremony, nor did I feel that god was present in that church building. I followed every prayer the priest said, drew the sign of the cross every time the names of Jesus and virgin Mary were mentioned. I listened carefully to the prayers sung by the choir, knelt and bowed when everyone did, listened to the sermon attentively, received Holy Communion with a serious feeling of humility, and placed some money in a basket when the service was about to end. I concluded that every liturgy I attended every Sunday morning was a formal ceremony without life and without spirit."

"How did this feeling come about? When?" my critic asked.

"I shall begin with the second part of your question. Is this agreeable with you?"

"Yes, why not? The two questions are interrelated."

"Well, this feeling began to creep into my mind when I was a young man. At first, it was indistinct and rather weak. I did not understand it or why I was having it until I began to mature intellectually and emotionally. This happened after I graduated from college. Possession of conceptual equipment and understanding of the fabric of culture in its moral, scientific, and philosophical dimensions is, I think, a necessary condition for this development. It was triggered by the prevalence of moral and religious

61

hypocrisy around me—my family members, friends, neighbors, relatives, even the priest and the bishop. They paid lip service to the values of the Eastern Orthodox church. What struck me as confusing, if not ironic, was that these values were used as a means to an end, and the end was personal advantage. The more I reflected on this phenomenon, the more I discerned that people weaved garments out of these values and wore them on demand. 'Beauty sells' is a popular saying in our society these days. But we can add to it another saying: 'religion sells.' It does not matter whether one is truly moral or religious; what matters is whether she appears moral or religious. Moral and religious values are stripped of their essential qualities and replaced by economic and hedonistic values.

"When I was still young, I frequently wondered: if these people existentially ignore the obligations entailed by these values, they necessarily deny faith in Jesus as the son of god; they equally deny belief in hell, heaven, last judgment, and the immortality of the soul; in short, they deny the basic doctrine of the church. Slowly, I came to the firm conclusion that they were followers of Caesar, not god. Coming to grips with this realization was not easy for me because I had to reconcile with the mask of hypocrisy people wore. Undertaking this reconciliation was like learning to sleep with one's enemy. But the enemy was formidable! Anyone who took these three values seriously was treated as naïve, weak, and stupid. I confess that I was treated this way. I always faced the ruthless dilemma: 'to be or not to be' true to myself. At first, I was not certain whether the values with which I identified myself were valid: why should I honor them and suffer ridicule and alienation from society if they were not valid?

"I lived in this fluid, indeterminate state of mind for a while, during which I never wavered from my commitment to those values. I simply felt that they were supremely important. Living according to them was consistent with the way I understood myself and life in general. Frankly, I felt at home with them. Gradually, I developed an attitude off indifference to social opinion, to how people viewed and treated me. Inner harmony can be a source of courage, hope, and strength. This state of indeterminacy was not transformed into a firm attitude until I plowed my way into the works of the philosophers, scientists, religious mystics of the East and the West, and the major novelists. Reading these works, which was always accompanied by long episodes of reflection on the nature of the world and the meaning of human life and destiny, awakened the *religious consciousness* that was dormant as a potentiality in my soul.

"By 'religious consciousness,' I do not mean consciousness of a religious object, idea, or image, but consciousness as a *mode of being*. The basis and object of this consciousness is a strong awareness of the presence of an ultimate being that underlies the existence and purpose of this whole scheme of the cosmos. The answer to questions such as 'Why does the universe exist?' and 'Why does it exist?' and 'How I should live?" laid within the folds of this consciousness."

"In your account of *the infinite* and the *religious consciousness*," my critic intervened, "the contemplation of the universe is a practice that can draw us closer to god. How does this kind of contemplation take place? The individual is, as you have pointed out more than once, *finite*, and so is the universe. How does she rise from her finite position or perspective, stand on the fringe of this perspective, and reflect on the vast realm of the universe? How can the finite being transcend her finitude? What prompts the individual to seek the source she cannot experience or the god she does not know in the first place? How would she recognize him if she succeeds in reaching it? I have discovered in the course of reading the history of human civilization that there are different ways of seeking god. What *daemon* inclined you to seek it?"

"Life!"

"Life?"

"Yes, nothing else."

"I asked for a brief answer, not a one-word answer," my critic said.

"Well, I shall try to be brief."

"Thank you!"

"The daemon that seduced me into a quest for god was, and remains, an intense passion for life, and by 'life,' I mean *human life, the kind of life that is worth living*."

"What makes a life worth living?"

"A life is worth living when it is lived according to the values that originate from the inner demands of human nature: goodness, beauty, and wisdom. These values are ideals, as I mentioned earlier. Each one of them embraces a cluster of subsidiary values. For example, justice, honesty, courage, love, or friendship originate from the ideal of goodness. Values such as elegance, grace, or splendor originate from the ideal of beauty. Values such as sound judgment, prudence, or truth originate from the ideal of wisdom.

"I discovered early on in my growth that designing my life-project according to these values should originate from one's mind and will, thoughtfully and purposefully. But then I asked myself, how should I live from my mind and will? Your life will be worth living if what you do in this world is worthwhile! This question led me to ask about the meaning of worthwhileness, that is, about what is *valuable or important*. But what makes an action or a life worthwhile? A large number of views loomed before my mind: pleasure, wealth, success, power, longevity, knowledge, glory, even immortality. I examined these views and concluded that the pursuit of goodness, beauty, and wisdom are the firmest basis of a worthwhile life."

"Now I see why you have been making frequent reference to these three values. But what made you settle on them?"

"If I am to be true to myself, I should live according to what I truly desire."

"What do you truly desire?""

These values derive their importance, indeed excellence, from the fact that living according to them meets the essential needs of human nature: they are values because they meet essential *human needs*. I desire long life, knowledge, pleasure, health, and success, but they do not meet the essential needs of our humanity. They are real needs, but they are not enough."

"What does humanity *essentially desire*?"

"It desires beauty, goodness, and wisdom—that is, love, truth, and skill in making sound judgments. If you possess these three virtues, then you can enjoy all the pleasure, success, health, wealth, or social respect you desire! How can you be healthy or successful if you cannot make sound judgments? How can your life be pleasant if you do not love someone who loves you? How can your life be cheerful and joyful if you do not delight in the beauty in nature, art, and human life?"

"Do you not think that your view of a worthwhile life is a bit idealistic and unrealistic?"

"Maybe yes, maybe no."

"What do you mean?"

"Ideals function as the rudder of human life. A boat without a rudder is a drifter. Likewise, a person whose life is without a rudder is a drifter. Next, ideals are not instruments or ready-made plans of action but *schemas,* and as such, they are a potentiality for infinite realization. There is always the possibility for richer, more meaningful realizations. *Our destiny as human beings is not to achieve perfection but to grow in perfection.* Growing in perfection is the ultimate source of true happiness! But the question that puzzled me, which I could not dismiss from my mind, was *why* I should lead a worthwhile life. This question was not fortuitous or whimsical; it sprang from a stubborn but disturbing fact: the pursuit of the ideals of human nature is a painful challenge. It involves struggle, frustration, and sometimes defeat. It is like ascending a rocky, dry, and tortuous mountain, the peak of which seems unreachable. Why should you choose this kind of life? Especially when you know that you have only one life to live and that that one life is short? Why not choose an easier way of life? Besides, to whom am I obligated to lead a worthwhile life? If only you know how many hours I have pondered these questions!

"The pursuit of goodness, beauty, and wisdom may seem idealistic, I know, but the question I faced was not whether my life was idealistic, realistic, or hard, but whether it was *worth living*. The only thing that would make it worth living, I thought, was whether or not the values on which it was built were justifiable. If these values were justifiable, then the obligation to live according to them is justifiable.

'But they spring from the essence of human nature!' a voice cried from within me.

'Yes, but is a life lived according to them justifiable if it is going to be a short and painful challenge?' I answered."

To tell the truth, that voice did not answer me. In the midst of looking for an answer, an invisible hand raised my vision upward: could it be that the human spark that shines in your heart and illuminates our vision of the ideals of goodness, wisdom, and beauty comes from a higher source, a source that justifies not only our existence but also these ideals? I know I exist; I also know that I am not the source of my existence. I might justify the pursuit of this or that end on the basis of a desire I feel, regardless of the source of this desire, but can I justify my own existence? For example, can I say that I deserve to exist, or that I have a right to exist? No. The basis of the justification of my own existence cannot be found within me but outside me.

"My quest for this basis gradually changed into a quest for the infinite: god. It was a slow, expansive process. You soon discover, as you proceed into it, that every object, be it physical or mental, is interconnected with a web of other objects that progress into infinity. And sooner or later, you also discover that the realm of reality is, as I mentioned to you in an earlier conversation, a *plenum*. The movement toward the infinite is like your movement from the first floor of a ten-story building to the last floor. You cannot ascend to the tenth floor in one step but by climbing the steps that lead to it. Likewise, you cannot reach the edge that overlooks the infinite in one step, which some people characterize as leap, but by penetrating, in an act of reflection, the domains that make up the structure of reality. Once your reflective intellect moves from one domain of reality to a wider domain, you are already on your way to the edge."

"Have you reached the edge? Have you stood on its ledge?" my critic asked.

I evaded these questions. I could not answer them. My lips trembled and then gave way to a soft smile. My critic's eyes, which were focused on my face, did not leave it; on the contrary, she sealed her lips with respectful silence as if to say, "Continue!"

"I believe that the ultimate source of passion for life—what gives us the strength, hope, and the courage to remain steadfast in the pursuit of our ideals despite the challenges and adversities we face in our endeavor to lead an authentic life—is a vision and a feeling of the radiance that emanates from the being of god. Once you have this kind of vision, you cannot anymore see the world the way you used to; you see it from the *standpoint of your vision of god*. You do not see your fellow human beings, regardless of their color, social status, religious belief, or ideology, as strangers or as others but as brothers and sisters in humanity. You do not anymore think of immortality or even of finitude because you live in the eternal now. And you do not fret about the possibility of adversity, because the whole phenomenon of death loses its significance. Moreover, you discover that the edge you stood on was not an edge, but that every point in the scheme of reality is an edge. You discover that you and the universe of which you are a part are continuous with the infinite depth of god. And most of all, you discover that the spark that shines in your heart and enables you to think, feel, and will derives its being and power from god."

My critic, who had been asking questions and listening to every word of my responses with critical and inquisitive eyes until this point, suddenly blushed and asked for a short break. "Please, accept my deepest apologies!" she said with a contrite expression on her face.

"Why?" I asked with a feeling of puzzlement.

"Well," she said, "I asked you to tell me how you met the fluteplayer. I felt an urgent need to make this request because your description of his character and music provoked in me an irrespirable desire to inquire about such a man. But then, unaware of what I was doing, I fired at you a barrage of questions that you kindly answered but that diverted you from your narrative about this unusual man. I now feel that I have taken an undue advantage of your generosity—"

"There is no need to apologize to me, please!" I said. "Conversing with you has been a source of deep satisfaction for me. Engaging with you in an intellectual conversation is a precious gift that I shall always cherish. I am grateful to you for this gift. Besides, the questions you fired at me were serious. I think we should not avoid the discussion of such questions. In fact, we might view this discussion as an introduction to my answer to your original question."

The expression of contrition that had covered her face a moment ago was transformed into one of amazement, of thoughtfulness. "Thank you!" she exclaimed. "I promise not to interrupt you again unless it is urgent."

"Every question asked is an urgently important question, at least to the person who asks it," I said in an attempt to make her feel as comfortable as possible.

She understood the purport of my response and added, "It might be good to take a lunch break. The sun left its zenith about an hour ago. You must be hungry. What do you think?"

"Yes, this is a good idea," I replied. I was about to invite her to lunch with me at Baudot's, but she intercepted my attempt.

"How about meeting again at 2:00 o'clock?" she said and left the rotunda through the western exist of the garden without giving me a chance to bid her goodbye.

The question of my critic's identity sprinted into my mind with unusual speed. "Does she eat?" I wondered. "Is she a human being? Is she real? I am real; theretofore, she should be real, otherwise, out conversations would not be real, but they are real. But goodness, she is acting like a real person would. Like a morally and culturally refined woman. Although these questions, which stormed my mind on more than one occasion, left a feeling of anxiety in it, as I was walking toward the parking lot, and although I felt an intense desire for answers, I kept my self-composure. Why should I worry so long as she did not do anything inappropriate or harmful? On the contrary, everything she did was proper, good, and highly valuable. Was I in the midst of a miracle or a miraculous situation? But I did not believe in miracles. "No," I thought, "I must be in the midst of a mysterious happening, one I do not understand yet but will."

My critic was standing at the western side of the rotunda between two columns, contemplating a weeping willow tree that sat next to a Prairie Cascade willow tree. Its long, slim branches were dancing gracefully in the wafts of a gentle breeze. She was unaware of my presence, and I did not disturb her; I simply stood at the lower landing of the stairway that led to the rotunda and contemplated the same tree. Weeping willow trees do not only weep, they also sing and dance. But to whom do they sing and dance, and for whom do they weep? I was unable to muse over these questions because my critic unexpectedly turned her body toward me and greeted me with a cheerful smile. She was angelic! I was not sure whether the face I was looking at was real or unreal.

"She must be a god-intoxicated woman, and she must have been singing a hymn to the infinite!" I whispered in the silence of my soul. But this whisper was drowned in the cheerfulness of her smile. Anyway, she was already seated on the bench when I was ascended the steps.

"How was your lunch?" she asked.

"It was good. Thank you!" I said. I really wanted to ask whether she, too, had eaten lunch or perhaps had just taken a restful break from the conversation. But I resisted the idea only because I felt that she was not interested in social talk.

She immediately asked, "How did you encounter the fluteplayer?" Then she added with a smile, "Indirectly?"

"As you will soon find out, it was truly indirect; nevertheless, it was a genuine encounter and perhaps more direct than the majority of encounters people usually have."

She smiled again but remained silent. Her silence gave me the needed time to resume my narrative.

"At first, soon after I began attending liturgy at St. John The Divine cathedral, I did not pay attention to the fluteplayer or to his music, thinking that he was a poor Jacksonian who was trying to make a living. This feeling was enforced by the fact that only a few of the churchgoers listened to his music. On a few occasions, I put some money in his benefaction basket without paying attention to his music. One day, a member of the congregation, who must have noticed that I was a new member, introduced himself to me as I was leaving the door of the sanctuary and engaged me in a rather long conversation. He desired to know where I lived before coming to Jackson, what I did, and whether I was a retired person. During this conversation, which was superficial and boring, I found myself listening to the music of the fluteplayer. To my surprise, it was not the kind of music I had often heard at a street corner, in the farmer's market, at parties, or in symphony halls. No, it was serious, spiritual, profound. It was the kind of music that steals your attention from the noise of the world and sends a waft of peace into your mind. A few times, I caught myself swallowing my saliva as I was trying my best to give the impression to the churchgoer that I was listening to him while in fact I was not. I felt guilty, but I could not prevent myself from listening to that music!

"Instead of going directly to my car, I stood next to the few people who were listening to the fluteplayer. Although my ears were captive to his music, my eyes were glued to the man playing it. The spiritual, regardless of whether it is a quality or an event, is not an ordinary object of perception. It takes a person with a spiritual bent of mind, a person with a spiritual appetite, to perceive and feel it. I was willing, indeed desirous, to rise to this spiritual opportunity, and I did. I confess that I could not extricate myself from the fluteplayer's music that morning until his audience, all except for an older woman who stood at his right side, had left the church grounds. Thinking that it was time for me to leave, I reluctantly proceeded to the benefaction basket, placed a rather generous donation in it, and left. I say 'reluctantly' because I really did not wish to part with that music! How could I have wished for it to end when every one of its tones and melodies poured the sweetest spiritual nectar into every fiber of my soul?

"Well, I did not anymore concern myself with the question of whether the liturgy was going to be an occasion of religious experience, whether the church building was a house of god, or whether the congregation was truly a community of religious people. I started to go to church every Sunday a little early only to listen to the fluteplayer's music and linger after the liturgy to hear his music again. I should, at this point of my answer to your question, underscore a significant fact: this alien, this anomaly, this enigmatic musician was an enchanter."

"An enchanter?" my critic cried, who was listening attentively.

"Yes, an enchanter!"

"What is the object of the enchantment he produced in his listeners?"

"You put your finger on the secret of this enchanter. The object of his enchanting music was not him or some idiosyncratic object or feeling because you do not see him or feel his presence. In fact, you do not see or feel anything natural or human, and you do not feel that you are in this world. Oh no, you feel that you are in a completely different world, in a world that transcends this one in beauty, mystery, and grandeur—in a world that is not illuminated by the light of our sun but by a sun that transcends every imaginable sun. You also feel that you are not the same person you were or hoped to be but a completely new person—ironically, without losing your identity.

"You see, unlike any other art, music streams into your heart and speaks to it directly. But the music of this man does not only speak to your heart, it enamors it and transports it to a world quite different from this world."

My critic, who had been listening intently to my account, suddenly put her two hands next to her hips and clutched the rim of the bench on which was sitting fiercely, as if she was trying to keep her body calm. I inadvertently noticed this change in her posture and was about to stop to see if she was ill at ease or if we were due for a short recess, but noticing my hesitation, she snapped, "Please, continue!"

Feeling assured that she was all right, I proceeded. "Yes, the music of this enchanter does not merely please or capture your heart with its charm but transports it to a world you have never seen, not even in the fairy tales of storytellers. Even though you feel that you are tethered to the ground of this Earth, you suddenly realize that the Earth on which this ground sits has glided into a different realm of being, one you cannot describe in any symbolic form. But at the same time, it is a world you can experience and comprehend, one whose existence you cannot doubt because although you stand in it, it envelops you with its light and caresses you with its warmth, one that makes you forget who you—not because your past self has ceased to exist, but because it has become what it should be.

"And, how can it become what it should be without this warmth? In the ordinary world, you are always thinking, desiring, worrying about this or that matter, and you are always struggling to solve this or that problem. But when you are enveloped by this warmth, you notice that you are not thinking, desiring, worrying, and struggling about this or that matter or problem, not because someone has removed them from your mind, but because you feel like you are *yourself*—because you feel complete. The powers of thinking, feeling, and willing remain active within you, but their activity shifts from the finite to the infinite. They focus their attention on the infinite. Instead of being filled with the mundane objects and matters of the world, now they are filled with the radiance of the infinite. But unlike the warmth of the sun, of your friend's presence, or your mother's lap, this warmth is addictive; you cannot live without it because you feel that your life *depends* on it. It creates in you an insistent inclination to feel it again and again. You soon realize that this warmth is the true nourishment you desire from your inmost being. You also realize that it is the source of your destiny. You realize that you are at home with yourself! Tell me, who wants to leave this kind of home?

"But this warmth is more thrilling, more magical, more alluring than you think, because once you feel it, once you feel you are enraptured by its seductive charm, you need more of it, not because you are greedy or selfish, but because it is absolutely valuable and so absolutely desirable. And you do not simply seek to have more of it but also to delve *into its source*, into the fire that gives rise to it. An appetite to be burned by this fire and sizzle in it surges into your heart and mind. People desire to sizzle in the *heat* of success, sex, love, pleasure, or victory over their enemy, and sure, they derive a special satisfaction from those things. But in desiring to sizzle in the fire of the infinite, you do not think of pleasure, thrill, glory, delight, even of joy. You think of something that surpasses any kind of enjoyment, any kind of experience, and any kind of meaning. You think of standing at the fountain of eternal creation, of contemplating its dynamics, of drinking from its life-giving nectar!"

"Have you stood at that fountain?" my critic asked, interrupting my train of thought. She must have been following every idea, every line of reasoning, every description I was relaying to her. But her eyes were wet—why? Could they have been wet if she were not a god-intoxicated woman? If she did not fully comprehend what I was saying? If she was not empathic in this comprehension? Alas! Did she need to be in the company of another god-intoxicated human being? I could not, and I did not, answer her question. Like I did when she had raised similar questions in our earlier conversations, I smiled. But let me hasten to add that my smile was not a social smile; it was intended to evade her question. It originated from a caring heart. I think she understood the meaning of it.

"Well," I said after some contemplation. "I became an addict to the fluteplayer's music, and I felt the nagging urge of my addiction sooner than I expected. Shortly after I began listening to him, I noticed that I was looking forward to the next Sunday morning. His image playing the flute began to intrude into my consciousness when I was performing my daily activities. More importantly, I felt a continual thirst for it. It might seem strange if I tell you that my interest in my daily activities, in my work at the college, even in my writing, which gave me profound satisfaction, was slowly fading. His image became a permanent fixture on the fringe of my consciousness. Gradually, it moved from its fringe to its center.

"Reluctantly, I tried to ignore it and focus my attention on my personal and professional duties, but I could not. So one Sunday, after his audience left, I approached the fluteplayer and tried to initiate a conversation with him. He did not respond to my greeting. As he did every Sunday when he stopped his music, he put his flute and his benefaction basket in his bag and rushed to his bicycle. The old woman who always stood by his right side watched me with bewildered eyes and abruptly left without saying a word to me.

"Why did he decline to speak to me? This question pricked my curiosity throughout the following week. But curiosity is a strange animal; it does not die easily. On the contrary, in my case, it grew in strength and persistence. Accordingly, next Sunday, as soon as he finished his playing, I rushed to the fluteplayer and greeted him very cordially. He ignored me. But I was determined to speak with him, so I softly tapped his shoulder as he was placing his flute in his bag. Then, I faced him and asked for a moment of his time. He gazed into my face thoughtfully, and without saying a word, he smiled. His smile was aglow with the music he played. Then he placed the benefaction basket in the bag and walked toward his bicycle. The old woman watched this scene silently. With an expression of tenderness in her eyes, she looked at me thoughtfully. Our eyes were locked in a silent conversation for a moment, but I decided to let this moment linger. I greeted her. Thankfully, she responded to my greeting genially. Without losing any time, I introduced myself to her. She smiled.

'You do not need to introduce yourself to me,' she said. 'I know you. I have been watching you listening to his music during the past few weeks.'

'Yes,' I said, 'I, too, have been watching you listen to his music. I have a strong, irresistible desire to speak with him, but he declined to speak with me. I wonder why?'

'He is deaf!'

'Deaf?' I almost screamed.

'Yes, he is deaf, but he is a gentle, lovable soul.'

'I cannot not doubt this testimony,' I thought to myself. 'The loveliness of his soul emanates from his music when his fingers dance on the flute. I wonder whether he knows how lovely, how noble, how uplifting, and how divine his music is. Does the genuine musician need to hear his music? Why should he hear it if it flows from his soul? Why should he doubt its nobility and its divinity if his soul is noble and divine? Why should his audience matter, when his music graces the space around him?'

I could not respond to the old woman's questions, but I looked at her with eager, baffled eyes. 'Who is she?' I wondered. 'Is she related to the fluteplayer? Is she one of his admirers or simply one of his audience members?' These questions flashed through my mind, but I did not have time to reflect on them.

'Are you one of them?' the old woman asked.

'Them? Who?' I replied with an expression of surprise on my face. 'Them!'

'I really do not know to whom you are referring,

'Do not be shy!' the old woman said. 'I can read it on your forehead!'

'What do you read? I cannot see my forehead.'

'Do you not see yourself in the mirror every morning when you brush your teeth and shave your beard and comb your hair?'

'I rarely see myself, much less my forehead, my teeth, my face, or my hair."

'You are one of them! This is exactly how they speak. People like you see without seeing and hear without hearing.'

'Your speech is oracular!' I cried.

'My speech might be oracular, but you are the oracle!'

'Are you trying to muddle my mind?'

'Your mind cannot be muddled, she said. 'I have never seen anyone who listens to his music the way you do.'

'How do I listen to it?' I asked. 'You see, I can neither see nor watch myself.'

'Why should you? Does the spring need to see or watch itself in order to be a spring?'

'Please, try not to evade my question: who is *them*?'

'Those who cannot see or even notice themselves. Those whose eyes are made to look in one direction.'

'What direction?'

'Upward."

'But I look in every direction—upward, downward, forward, and backward.'

'But for *them—for you*—every direction is an upward direction. Those who look upward are enchanted by the light of the infinite the way ordinary people are enchanted by the light of the sun. They are captives to this light. They cannot live without it; they constantly gravitate toward it.'

'You do not know me. How can you speak this way about me?'

'I have just met you, yes, but everything I said about you is written on your forehead. Unfortunately, the greatest majority of people cannot read. You can, but you do not need to read. The script I read says that you are one of them.'

'But if you can read this script, you, too, must be one of them.'

'What you say is logical but does not reflect the facts. A scholar in physics or philosophy is not necessarily a physicist or a philosopher.'

'But how can you be such a scholar if you do not know what it is like to be a physicist or a philosopher?'

"The old woman did not respond to my question but looked into my eyes reflectively, compassionately. I felt her compassion. I also felt that she pretended to be a scholar not because she was a dishonest or a deceptive woman but because she was shy about revealing her true identity. Otherwise, why did she always stand by the right side of the fluteplayer? And why did she attend all of his recitals regularly? Why did she feel free to engage me in a conversation about god-intoxicated people? No, she too must be one of them.

"Compassion still flowing from her face when she moved one step closer to me and said, 'I look forward, with anticipation, to seeing you next Sunday.' Then, she disappeared from my presence.

"I stood alone next to the stairway that led to the cathedral for a long time, thinking about my encounter with the old woman. It was clear to me that the word 'them' meant god-intoxicated people. But why did she refer to them as a group? Are they organized into some kind of society or association? Impossible! Why should they be? Such people are free spirits. They live in the world, but they are indifferent to its ways and pursuits. They love it because it is blessed by the hand of god. They promote human ideals because they originate from the human essence, and they devote themselves to their fellow human beings because they are divine sparkles. Oh, how many a god-intoxicated person walks in the streets of life incognito? No, such people do not need to organize themselves into an association, because they live from the inner sparkle that shines in their hearts. Because they derive their purpose, courage, hope, and vision of life from that sparkle.

"But then, why did the old woman refer to them as 'them' as if they were members of an association? Yes, they must be a group, and they can be identified as a *kind of group*, of course informally, because they exhibit, in the way they act and express themselves, the same spirit that animates their lives. Suppose one is an American, Chinese, or Indian citizen—do we not identify her cultural identity by the way she acts and expresses herself in the world?

"Broadly speaking, do we not reflect the spirit of the culture that flows in our veins by the way we act and express ourselves in the different domains of human life? Do we not feel affinity with members of our culture when we are abroad? Why should it be strange, then, for a god-intoxicated person, one who lives from the divine spark within, to identify another god-intoxicated person? Why should it be strange to have a feeling of kinship with her even when we meet her for the first time? And why should it be strange to form a mutual bond of solidarity when we interact with someone so likeminded?

"I could not refrain from musing on this phenomenon when I walked toward the parking lot. It was empty, and so were the adjacent streets, but my soul was not. Every fiber of my being was celebrating the divine ritual the fluteplayer performed in the open space of the church building. A large number of the congregation usually ate lunch at some restaurant after they celebrated Holy Communion, but I did not go to any restaurant. Frankly, I did not eat lunch at all that day. I did not need to eat because I felt fulfilled. My mind, heart, and body were in complete harmony. The enriching effect of the fluteplayer, which was enforced by my encounter with the old woman, refused to leave me. Its power was mesmerizing, transportive, uplifting; it was a life-giving power. In this state of mind, you feel that you are in a different world, on the edge. You feel you are in the presence of the divine.

"I lived in the light of this presence, albeit impatiently, until the following Sunday. The image of the fluteplayer and the old woman standing by his right side hovered on the rim of my mind as I was driving my car to the cathedral the next weekend. Unawares, I found myself singing Beethoven's "Ode to Joy." The song flowed from my mouth spontaneously. I smiled! The expectation of seeing someone dear or significant always stirs deep and warm emotions in us. I was bubbling with these emotions when I parked my car and walked toward the fluteplayer's 'recital hall.' But, to my surprise, the hall was empty. Neither the fluteplayer, nor the old woman, nor anyone else was there. I was baffled, sad, and disappointed. I stood in the vacant space and looked around, hoping to see someone, but I did not. The vacant space that enfolded me was oppressive, very oppressive. I remained in the same spot for a few more minutes, still hoping that the fluteplayer or the old woman would come. Desire frequently gives rise to hope, but my desire was not fulfilled.

"'Is he sick?' I wondered. 'Is he in some kind of trouble?' When people charge into their seventies, they become targets of accident and health issues. But the old woman did not come, either—why? 'Is she with him,' I wondered, 'or perhaps attending to him? Is she his friend?'

"Like a bee hopping from one flower to another, I was hopping from one question to another. Honestly, I was restless! But I could not hop over questions for a long time because the faithful were already streaming into the sanctuary of the cathedral. I joined them but stood next to the entrance of the church building. I entertained the possibility of seeing the old woman among the worshippers. She was not there! Goodness! Why could she be there? What god-intoxicated person would be there? And why should I be there?

'Are you an idol worshipper?' I asked myself.

'No!' I responded, silently.

And yet, I remained transfixed in my spot, not because I was worshipping the Christian god but because I was hoping to see the old woman or hear the music of the fluteplayer.'

"But neither the fluteplayer nor the old woman came to church that morning. I waited in that recital hall until everyone departed. Two persons, who must have recognized me as one of the fluteplayer's audience, greeted me with a smile but did not stop to chat with me. I wondered whether they missed the recital, too. I felt lonely—lonely for the fluteplayer, for his music, and in a different way, lonely for the old woman. And yet, in spite of this painful feeling, I continued to attend liturgy regularly, hoping that I might see the old woman and perhaps the fluteplayer again.'

"One Sunday, after a few months of living with this loneliness, I noticed, with a shock, that the old woman was standing at the landing of the stairway with her back to the entrance of the church. She was gazing into the sky. With anxious mind and heavy heart, I rushed to her side. She did not notice me at first, maybe because she was lost to the infinity of the space, but she must have felt my presence. The warmth of human presence speaks more articulately, more directly, more confidently, and more significantly than any other type of human communication. Slowly but confidently, the old woman turned her face toward me and cast a compassionate, consoling look into my eyes.

"She did not speak at first, but a few moments later, she asked me to descend the stairway with her. I did.

'He will not sing anymore—' she said. She paused and then added, 'Not to us!'

"My heart began to pound against the wall of my chest cavity, and the blood flowed in my veins the way a cataract flows through a rocky gorge.

'When? How?' I blurted out, unable to control myself.

'Two months ago. I do not know how or why he decided to stop singing. A few days after we met, I purchased some groceries for him and placed them, as I always did, at the doorstep of his cottage and left.'

'You did not knock at the door?'

'No, I never did. In fact, I never entered his cottage or paid him as visit. I began the practice of buying fruits, vegetables, bread, and the basic ingredients he'd need to cook decent meals and placing them at the doorstep of his cottage. He must have accepted them, because whenever I placed the new bag of supplies at the doorstep, I noticed that the previous bag was not there. It was not hard for me to infer that he was accepting my donation.'

'Have you ever spoken with him?' I asked again.

'No, never!'

'Did he know that you were the one who used to place the bag of groceries at his doorstep?'

'It did not matter whether or not he knew the identity of the donor. What mattered is that he accepted them.'

'You have never spoken with him?' I asked again.

'Never! Did I need to speak with him? Listening to his music was the only conversation I desired.'

'I understand. Yes, I truly understand what you mean. But as far as I know, you have always stood at his right side. Could it be that he knew that you were his benefactor?'

'I cannot answer your question, but I can assure you that he was oblivious to me, to his audience, and to the churchgoers when he sang. I stood at his right side because, ironically, I did not want him to notice me. But I had a strong desire to be as close to him as possible. He was a center of gravity, and I could not help but gravitate toward him. The warmth that emanated from his music was home for me.'

"I could not divert my eyes from the old woman's face. I was anxious to know more about the fluteplayer, and if possible, about his life.

'But how did you know where he lived?'

'He always rushed to his bicycle, mounted it, and vanished from my sight with the speed of light. So, one Sunday, anxious to know where he lived, I brought my bicycle with me and parked it at the eastern side of the cathedral. Just before he was about to depart, I sped to my bicycle and followed him, for I did not want him to notice me. Well, let me tell you that he lived in a small cottage on the eastern side of Lambeth Woods. Hardly anyone goes to that area because it is densely covered with trees and bushes. It is difficult to ride a bicycle through the trees, so I used to park my bicycle at the rim of the woods and walk to his cottage with my grocery bags.'

'How did he die? How did you discover his departure of this world?'

'Two weeks after I noticed that he had not removed the most recent grocery bag from the doorstep, I knocked at his door, thinking that there might be somebody there. There was no answer. I knocked again, and again, there was no answer. I knew he was deaf. I was worried. Impulsively, I knocked at the door several times, even though I knew he was deaf. Then I turned the knob of his door, and it responded to my attempt. Apparently, he was not in the habit of locking his door. I let myself in. The cottage was composed of one room and a kitchen. A small cot, a chest of drawers, and two straw chairs filled the room. The bag that contained his flute and the benefaction basket were next to the cot. Although it was a poor man's cottage, it was clean and neatly organized. One small window was open.

'He was lying on his back. His body was covered with a deep red blanket. A flood of light was flowing from the window onto his face. Although he had clearly been dead for some time, his complexion seemed fresh and lifelike. His mouth and eyes were closed. His hands were under the blanket. He must have left the world voluntarily because I could not detect any sign of violence on him or around the cot. I was shocked when I stood next to him and watched his peaceful, angelic face. I wished I could remain next to him forever! Who would not have this wish? I had a strong desire to go to the bag, only because I wished to feel the flute. It was silent, and its silence was serenely sad! Tears flooded my eyes; they were interrupted by audible, mournful sobs. Tears rolled down my cheeks and landed on the blanket that covered his body. I wonder whether he felt them, but I think he did.'

"The eyes of the old woman were wet when she uttered the last sentence. I understood the depth of her sorrow and sympathized with her. The tears that rolled down her checks and found their way to the blanket were not only tears of sorrow; they were tears of love, of appreciation, of loyalty to the divine light that emanated from the flute of that enigmatic man!'

'And then?' I impulsively asked. The old woman had lost herself in a long spell of reflection, as if she was having a silent dialogue with the spirit of the fluteplayer.

'And then?' she said, extricating herself from the spell with some effort. 'I called the police. Three officers arrived at the cottage within half an hour. They asked me several questions about the dead man—what he did, whether he had any friends or relatives, and what relationship I had with him. They also asked some questions about me. They inspected the cottage carefully.

'*Nothing!* one of them said after they completed their inspection.

'*Strange!* another officer said as he wrote his report. *I just do not understand how this man lived and how he died. The corpse does not even smell bad. There is hardly anything in this shack!*

'*Wait a moment!* the second officer said after he looked under the cot. *There is a suitcase here.* He opened it. It contained several bundles of papers. Two of them were handwritten manuscripts. He examined them and then said, *No legal documents. He must have been a philosopher. This is what his vitae says. He must have been a teacher. Odd!*

'*You should have these papers and documents,* the officer said to me. *They look academic to me. I doubt that anyone would be interested in them.* He showed the documents to the first officer, who examined them and then said, *Yes, they should belong to you.*

'When the police officers completed their inspection and called the hospital. they recommended that I leave the cottage. *There is no need for you to stay here, ma'am,* one officer said. *We shall wait for the ambulance.*

'Well, I went back to my apartment and remained secluded there until the next morning. I was not grieving because there was no need to grieve; I was simply trying to adjust to his absence, even though he was not, and is not, absent, because it is impossible for a man like him to leave you once he smites you with the flame of his love. I examined all the documents from his suitcase. He was a philosopher, but more importantly, he was an artist of the human soul. I have a feeling that anyone, even a philosopher, who touches the finger of god becomes an artist. You can teach a person the various techniques of art-making, but you cannot teach her how to become an artist—that is, how to capture the truth and express it in symbolic form. I now think that the aim of philosophy is not merely to create a philosophical system or even to interpret the world in a certain way but to enable the system or the interpretation to shine with the truth of what underlies the world.

'One of the bundles of the papers the officer had not opened contained an envelope. I opened it. It included a note and a bank statement from Jackson Trust Bank. The statement showed a balance of $210,500. The note said that this sum should be awarded as a gift to the philosophy department at Lambeth College. He signed the note as *James Amore.*

'I am not proficient in financial matters,' she said to me, taking the envelop out of her pocket. We were still standing in the cathedral stairwell, but my mind was lightyears away. 'Would you please execute his will?' She gave me the envelope and the other papers. I read the two short manuscripts he left. You should read them, too.'

'Gladly,' I said.

'This morning,' the old woman said, 'I felt a strong urge to come here. Not to attend liturgy but to see you. I was not certain that I would see you in the sanctuary because you are not an idolater, but I thought I might in the invisible concert hall of the fluteplayer.'

'I have been coming to this place regularly because I missed you and felt an overwhelming desire to feel your presence,' I said. 'Can we meet again?'

'Of course. Nobody knows whether we, or one of us, might learn to sing the way the fluteplayer did.'

"I did not respond to this remark but let a soft smile dance on my lips. She noticed it and smiled, too. We agreed to meet again in the invisible concert hall of the fluteplayer. Before leaving, she pulled another manuscript out of her handbag and gave it to me.

'You should read it,' she said. 'I believe you will find it interesting, provocative. You are a philosopher. Do with it what you see appropriate. I think it is a proper sequel to our conversation.'

"Although I met the old woman a few times after that, I have since lost contact with her. She suddenly stopped coming to the invisible recital hall. I was unable to reestablish any kind of contact with her because she declined to give me her address or telephone number. I only wish to goodness that she was not another fluteplayer!"

"What if she were?" my critic asked.

"I would have liked to listen to her music!"

"Have you read the manuscript?"

"Yes, I have. It is a fascinating account of the fluteplayer's meeting with god."

"With god?"

"Yes!"

"I would very much like to read it."

"Wonderful! Can we meet again to discuss it?"

"Nothing is more delightful to me than to share my heart and mind with a person who welcomes me into her presence."

"Are you sure?" my critic said, smiling. Then, she vanished from my presence. She did not appear in it again. Questions about her identity slowly faded from my memory, but I missed her. These questions did not matter anymore. What mattered and I what I cherished for the rest of my life was the light she left in my heart.

The following chapters were written by the fluteplayer. Please, dear reader, treat them as a sequel to the conversations I presented in the preceding chapters.

Chapter Five

The Fluteplayer
Ascends the Peakless Mountain

W HEN I was a young man, my grandmother used to call me Stargazer, most likely because I was enchanted by the sun. I used to wake up at dawn and watch the sun slowly rising from behind the eastern horizon and slowly illuminating our planet with its light, and I used to watch it at dusk, too, slowly setting behind the western horizon, leaving behind a blanket of darkness. I always desired to know how it produced its rays and filled the world with light—how it moved from one side of the horizon to the other every day, and how this cycle continued so rhythmically.

I also desired to know the nature and meaning of this mysterious cycle: can life, even the world as we know it, exist without the sun? If we wipe out light from the world, total darkness will certainly prevail. Can anything exist or thrive in the dark? Can we perceive any type of form in the dark? Some scientists theorize about the Big Bang explosion—that we can conceive the existence of pure matter in some kind of darkness. But by what means can we claim any knowledge of a formless object or of any type of reality? A formless object is an indescribable object, and an indescribable object is an unknowable object. I confess that I can neither perceive nor conceive any type of object that exists or thrives in the dark.

Although at first I felt it indistinctly, I felt that light was the source of life and the world, and that it is also the power that makes them endure. Reality continues to exist as long as light continues to exist: if light ceases to exist, reality collapses into nonexistence. This conclusion may seem naïve, but it is not, because it entails recalcitrant ramifications. As some physicists have pointed out, it is possible for our sun to die out. If this happens, our stellar system will certainly collapse. This shows that our stellar system and every object in the universe is contingent and unnecessary in the sense that they exist but *do not have to exist.*

Moreover, these objects are not self-created but depend, for their existence, on some agent or power that is external and superior to them. But if every object in the universe is contingent, it is, I think, reasonable to say that the universe itself is contingent; and if it is contingent, then a power external to it must be its source. This power must, by necessity, be luminous. Accordingly, a sun must be the source of all the suns in the universe and consequently of the order and the life that thrives in it.

This or that sun comes into being while another passes out of being, and so the universe might undergo a continual process of transformation—in short, change might remain king. But this king and the universe it governs can neither exist nor continue to exist without assuming the existence of a permanent sun, the luminosity of which transcends the luminosity of every conceivable sun the human mind can imagine. But then, if sunlight is the power that animates the universe, if it is the source of the gravity that keeps it up—in short, if the universe can neither exist nor continue to exist without it—it should follow that the universe is an emanation from the *ultimate sun,* exactly the way light is.

This relationship between the sun and our planet and between the universe and the necessary existence of an ultimate sun, which was, at first, indistinct in my mind, gradually took hold of my imagination and lurked in my subconscious mind as a kind of quiet urge. I kept this urge a secret, mainly because if I disclosed it to my friends or family members, and even to my science teacher, it would have exposed me to the charge of lunacy.

I would frequently wake up early in the morning and contemplate the gradual rise and procession of the sun toward its zenith and wonder about its reason for being. Its journey from the eastern to the western horizon was, to my mind, astonishing, majestic. Please, contemplate this glowing, golden disk as it makes its lonely journey into infinite space and then, emerging from it, returns, again and again. Contemplate yourself watching this glorious procession, if possible, and then ask for the reason for being of this glorious scene! As a young man whose imagination was still a burst of curiosity, creativity, and desire for knowledge, I could not refrain from allowing my mind to probe not only this mysterious procession but also its author—the sun.

One day, my grandmother, who must have been cognizant of my adventures with the sun, paid me a visit soon after I had returned from school for the day.

"Those who gaze into the sun, my dear," she said after she inquired about my school work and personal life and made sure that I was doing well in both, "are bound to fall in love with it. They say that its beauty and sublimity transcend in their magnificence the beauty and sublimity of any beautiful and sublime objects human beings have ever witnessed in this whole wide universe. It is so powerful, so alluring, no one can resist it, and once a person is enamored by it, she cannot extricate herself from its allure. She cannot anymore live without it. She thrives on watching it, and without it, she languishes into severe depression.

"But I think there is more to it, much more, than its beauty and sublimity. There is something mysterious, something magical, something delicious and mesmerizing that draws a person to it. I do not know what it is, and I have not heard any man or woman describe it, although I once heard one man allude to it vaguely and reluctantly. I think he refrained from describing it not because he was shy or afraid, for such lovers are never afraid of anything, but because he did not know how to say it. The real 'thing,' he emphasized to me, is that once you fall in love with the Earthly sun, you cannot stop there; your mind looks beyond our golden disk to the ultimate sun, to the source that makes the Earthly sun radiant with light.

"But what baffles my mind, my dear," my grandmother continued, "is that not many people who fall in love with the sun and who pursue it with sincere desire, and I can say passion, return the same persons after they encounter it. After they feel the warmth of its arms. After they drink a cup of its nectar. One woman, who declined to say a word about it, confessed that once you drink that cup, you become drunk forever. She insisted that I should take her words metaphorically. Having stared into my eyes for a moment, she added rhetorically, 'How can a blind woman describe what she sees, especially after she feels the warmth of those arms? Did someone tell you that blind people see more clearly, more truthfully, than people with excellent vision do? Did your Oedipus not see more, much more than any human being ever had after he was blinded? Did he not see the truth he was seeking with the great possible clarity *after* he was blinded?' Like many drunkards, these blind people speak paradoxically! You have to analyze their words carefully if you want to understand them.

"Falling in love with a man or a woman is not easy; it is one of the most daunting challenges human beings face. Can you imagine how difficult it would be to fall in love with the true sun? Loving this goddess (and all sun lovers refer to it as a *goddess)*, is a process of delving deep into her heart, but her heart is different from the heart of any human being. No one can describe it, but all those who have paid a visit to it say that it is an infinite ocean of love! They say that it requires extensive understanding of nature and human nature, a passionate desire for it, and a firm determination to drink a cup of that nectar.

"No one who has paid a visit to the sun regretted her encounter with it. An old man who came back from such a visit a little while ago confided to me that the different faces of beauty we carve when we contemplate the sun from our Earthly point of view are nothing, practically meaningless, compared to the splendor, exuberance, and grandeur of the beauty of the *true sun*—the sun that gives rise to all the suns that punctuate the heavenly sky. It surpasses the beauty of anything your mind can imagine." My grandmother paused for a few seconds and then added, "Not every human being can fall in love with the sun, my dear. You should not gaze into it if you are not certain that loving it is what you truly desire. Otherwise, you will damage your vision. You will be in college next year. You will have ample time to think about this project."

"Have you been in love with the true sun, grandmother?" I could not help but ask.

"You should not ask an old woman this kind of question, my dear!"

"But you seem to know so much about the sun and sun lovers. I have never met any person who knows about it or who has had an encounter with it," I responded with a loving smile on my face.

"I told you not to ask an old woman such questions," she retorted with an equally loving smile on her face.

Seeing that she was reluctant to answer my question, I asked another. "How does one seek an encounter with the sun?"

"The way a person seeks an encounter with his or he beloved. If you love the sun, you should pay her a visit and tell her how you feel about her."

"How? Is there a way?"

"A number of sun lovers who have had an encounter with it speak of a *peakless mountain*. Anyone who seeks such an encounter should ascend this mountain all the way to the top or somewhere near the top. Once you reach this spot, you will know—you will know everything you need to know."

"Peakless mountain?" I blurted with unbelieving eyes.

"Yes, the mountain they mentioned is peakless. You will recognize it when you reach its foot."

"But how can a peakless mountain be a mountain?" I pressed.

My grandmother gaped into my eyes intently and added, "Not everything in our life, my dear, is governed by the logic of the philosopher. There is a higher logic. All contradictions, all paradoxes, all mysteries melt in the heat of the sun."

Although I did not understand what my grandmother said, I asked, "Where is the peakless mountain?"

"It lies somewhere north of the Great Smokey Mountains. You should not think of such details, though, and more importantly, you should stay away from the sun. If you impair your vision now, you will not be able to see your way in your life. This is my advice." She left the room.

Although I loved and respected my grandmother immensely, sometimes to the point of reverence, I could not heed her advice. Some secret power, perhaps my *daemon*, propelled me to keep contemplating the sun every dawn and every dusk. I was not only curious about the beauty and mystery that oozed out of it, which I enjoyed with every fiber of my being, but also—and perhaps especially—about the source of this beauty and mystery. My grandmother spoke of a *higher sun* as the source of all the suns in the universe. If she was correct, and I think she was, then the source of the Earthly sun should be more beautiful, more sublime, more magnificent, and therefore more desirable than the beauty, sublimity, and magnificence of the earthly sun. The more I probed the dynamics of this phenomenon, the more I was determined to pursue the *ultimate sun* as the supreme goal of my life. I desired to have an encounter with it!

This passion did not abate but on the contrary grew in magnitude, especially when I explored the realms of art, science, and philosophy a few years later. The eyes of my imagination never left the sight of the sun during this exploration. I was amused when I took a course in geology and read in my textbook that the sun is a big ball of fire—a huge mass of energy. This discovery intensified my interest in the sun; its very existence pointed to a being that surpassed it in power and beauty. Most if not all of the major works I read in philosophy and literature, the artworks I studied in depth, and the works I experienced in symphony halls, museums, and theaters reinforced this conclusion. The more I surrendered myself to philosophical contemplation, especially after I received my terminal degree in philosophy, and the more I did research and taught in that field of knowledge, the more intense was my passion to have an encounter with it. This passion became a living flame at the height of my adult life. When such a flame kindles in your mind, you cannot ignore it. I could not, and I did not.

With a peaceful state of mind, a state I had never experienced in my life, I decided to ascend the peakless mountain my grandmother had told me about. Is it possible that all of those philosophical and artistic minds who sought to know about the sun that transcends every other sun and every object in the universe and the universe itself, not to mention those men and women who claimed to have had encounters with it, were misguided? That they were fools? Is it possible that the wisdom that underlies the whole phenomenon of religion, from the earliest period of human civilization to the present has been a lie?

An irrepressible consciousness rose from the depth of my being and cried, "No!" Truly, every beat of my heart endorsed this cry. I felt like I was on fire when I delivered my lectures at the college, that I was walking on fire wherever I went, and that I was lying in a bed of fire when I slept. I was aflame with fire—with the fire of my passion for the sun!

I strongly wished, and this wish was a frequent visitor of my mind, that I had pressed my grandmother for details about the peakless mountain when I was making my plan to ascend it. How could I plan such trip if I did not exactly know where I was going? And yet, I knew. The Great Smokey Mountains are real. If all the sun lovers who ascended it found it, I should find it and I should ascend it. I ruminated on this and other ideas soon after I occupied my seat on the bus to Mountain City.

"Do not make a hasty decision, my dear," my grandmother reminded me when she was on her death bed. "The sun can blind your eyes. But if it does not blind them, then you will be able to see clearly, more clearly than you might wish!"

This thought reverberated in my mind more than any other thought did. The warmth of her hand that clasped mine tightly after she made this remark lingered in my heart to this moment.

"Was she a lover of the sun?" I wondered. "But, alas, who could have spoken about it and its devotees the way she did if she was not such a lover?" Unawares, I felt that my heart was heaving heavily. "Yes, she must have been!" I mumbled as the bus traversed the winding roads of the Tennessee mountains.

It was almost dusk when I left the Greyhound bus station at Mountain City, so I decided to spend the night in that town. A small, rather neglected motel stood next to the station. There was no need for me to hire a taxi, so I walked the distance. An elderly woman received me with a warm welcome and a reserved, rustic smile on her lips.

"Can I have a room for he night?" I asked after I placed my heavy knapsack on the floor next to the reception desk.

"Yes, sir, you certainly can!" she said and then asked for my identification and credit cards. I inquired about an eating place.

"We do not have a dining room here, but there is a nice restaurant down the road. You cannot miss it. It is the only restaurant in town."

I thanked her and then went to my room. I took a bath and then went to the restaurant. My room was simple but clean, and the meal I ate at the restaurant was simple but wholesome.

The same elderly woman was at the counter when I came to the office to check out on the following morning. An elderly gentleman, most likely her husband, was sitting at a high chair next to her.

"I hope the room was to your liking?" the lady asked.

"Yes, ma'am, it was. It is peaceful around here."

"We are country folks. We live close to nature and with it. We like it. We live a very simple but honest life."

"This is the kind of life everybody should live, I think, but honesty is not as common as we might think it is."

"Unfortunately, you are right," she said, handing me my receipt.

"Do you happen to know the way to the peakless mountain?" I asked before departing the motel.

"The peakless mountain?" she asked with a thoughtful frown on her face and then shook her head sideways. She turned to her husband. "Honey, do you know the way to the—?" She paused for a second and then looking at me intently, she asked, "What mountain?"

"The peakless mountain."

"Do you know the way to the peakless mountain, honey?"

Her husband did not answer her question promptly, but after casting a long, scrutinizing look at me, he said, "Take Highway 91 to Laurel Bloomberry. When you arrive at the tri-state meeting point, ask the driver to let you out. No one knows where its foot is, but it is somewhere in that area. Be careful. They say that the terrain is rough, hostile, forbidding. Good luck!"

"Thank you very much!"

"He is one of them loonies," I overheard him whisper rather audibly to his wife as I was leaving.

One of them loonies! Labeling me as a loony did not offend me. If those who loved the true sun were loonies, I was very pleased to be one. In fact, being called a looney and referred to as "one of them" implied to me that my grandmother was right. "This mountain exists," I told myself, "and it exists in this region." This realization sent a waft of peace into my mind.

As soon as the bus driver locked up the luggage compartment and was about to move to his next destination, I asked whether he would let me out at the tri-intersection point.

"There?" he asked with an expression of amazement on his face.

"Yes, sir!"

"As far as I know, there are no towns or settlements in that area. Are you sure this is where you wish to leave the bus?"

"Yes, sir."

"Sure thing!" the driver said, curling his lower lip inward. He shook his head sideways and cast one more look at me without saying a word. Then he examined the seats to determine whether all the passengers were in. They were.

True to his word, the driver stopped at the tri-state intersection point. "Are you sure this is your destination?" he asked as I was leaving the bus.

"Thank you very much! Yes, this is my destination."

The driver threw a compassionate look at me. "Do you have a head-gear?" he asked.

"Headgear?" I wondered with a feeling of puzzlement.

"It is going to be very hot. You will need a hat to protect your head from the sun; it is scorching hot today. You do not need a sun stroke, not in this god-forsaken place."

I was embarrassed, so I remained silent. The bus driver left his steering wheel, went to the luggage compartment, and returned with a wide-rimmed hat. "Wear this!" he said kindly. The feeling of embarrassment, which was already reeling fiercely in my heart, became so intense that I almost cried, not only for the gift of compassion but also for my naiveté. I accepted the gift and thanked him profusely for his generosity and kindness. A gift that originates from the human heart is the most precious gift we give and receive in this world, I think.

The man at the motel was right. The terrain my eyes surveyed when I stood alone on the side of the road was rugged. It was punctuated with small hills and mounds covered with low-growing plants. It was surrounded by a range of high mountains. I felt like I was standing on a big plate carved by nature. But I was not interested in that range or in any of its mountains. The mountain I was seeking was peakless, higher than any of the peaks that sat on it, one that spiraled upward toward the sun.

Without losing any time, I followed the track I had charted in my mind as I was surveying the terrain, but the patch I chose was not straight, and it was not easy to traverse because the ground was covered with bushes, rocks, marshes, streams, and water running down from the foot of the range. But this ruggedness did not deter my will or fervor, for I was burning with desire to feel the light of the sun, the sun my mind and heart has been longing for ever since I was a young man. Ironically, the Earthly sun, the sun the bus driver warned me about, was burning hot. The hat he gave me as a gift was always on my head; in fact, I kept it there even when I was in the shade! I had to take several breaks to rest and drink water during the day.

The configuration of the terrain around me remained practically the same throughout the first day of my trip, and yet, it was necessary for me to scan the land that stretched before my eyes and choose the most feasible track to move onward. I felt somewhat tired when the sun approached the mountain range. I knew I should locate a safe place for the night—but where? Under a tree? In a cave? In a thick, sturdy bush? That was my first adventure into the wild. I suddenly realized that I had travelled into the mountains without sufficient planning, knowledge, or experience. Desire, faith, enthusiasm, clarity of purpose, and courage are not enough. One should also possess practical skills when undertaking such an adventure. To my painful surprise, I did not have such skills. But again, need, especially the need for survival, is sometimes a source of invention.

Because there were no caves, trees, or thick bushes, I began looking for a hill. "The larger the hill, the greater the possibility of discovering or creating a shelter in it or around it," I thought. I spotted one and walked toward it. Although I had not been mistaken in choosing this hill, neither discovering nor creating a shelter in it was easy. Rain and snow had dug a reasonably large notch on its western side. I decided to transform the notch into a shelter. Toward that end, I uprooted some shrubs and collected several branches and placed them next to the notch. Then, I looked for wild fruits in the vicinity and was shocked out of my wits when I discovered some blueberry plants. I tasted one of them to make sure that it was not poisonous. It was sweet as honey! I plucked as many berries as I could and saved some of them for a meal I had already packed in my knapsack. I saved the rest for the following day. Although the meal I ate was modest, it was satisfactory; indeed, I enjoyed it

When the sun began to gather its golden rays back from our planet, I created a grid-like formation out of the dead branches and covered it with as many bushes as I could. I used some sticks as spikes to keep the grid in place. Then, I closed the opening with the remainder of the bushes. No animals came close to my "hut" during the night. The only sign of animal life I was able to detect was when I heard Coyote howls coming from afar. My sleep was peaceful. The only thing I regretted when I woke up next morning was my failure to take a bath in one of the streams I crossed the day before. I have always enjoyed taking a bath. This habit never left me to the last day of my life.

Frankly, I was so intent on finding the foot of the peakless mountain that I had hardly paid attention to my needs or to what I should expect on the following day or days. I confess that I was totally ignorant of the nature of my adventure. The only thing I knew with certainty was the supreme value of my purpose and my absolute faith in it—that the peakless mountain was the way that led to the sun. The question of what it would take to reach the peakless mountain and ascend it, what might be involved in ascending it, how I would reach a peakless point, much less a peakless mountain, whether I would be able to withstand the adversities that might befall me—these and similar questions were not on mind. I was a man on a mission, and I pursued it with the zeal of a believing disciple!

You will certainly think that I was a naïve, impulsive, and perhaps a dumb person, and you might admonish me for my hastiness, for yielding to my impulse, and for not acting according to the rules of reason, especially because I was a philosopher and supposedly committed to the rational way of thinking and acting. I deserve your admonishment. But please, view me as a man in pursuit of a supremely valuable cause, as a man who was trying to explore the road to his destiny, as a man who was trying to meet the sun of all suns, the source of the universe—of my destiny and yours!

When your intellect is dominated by this spiritual posture, you do not think of what people say or of the misfortunates that may befall you. You simply pursue your goal with a feeling of confidence and determination, and you face any danger, difficulty, or challenge with a reasonable degree of modesty, understanding, and patience. You gradually discover that human nature is resourceful, that nature is not as hostile as some people have portrayed it as being, and that accomplishing worthwhile purposes is, much of the time, humanly possible.

The golden rays of the sun, which glided through small openings of the roof I had created over my head, woke me up the following morning with a gentle kiss on my eyes! Oh, how lovely were those rays! Before resuming my trip to the peakless mountain, I went to the blueberry bush. It was loaded! I plucked a large amount of fruit, ate some, and saved the rest for the evening. With the aid of my compass, I proceeded northward, always making certain that I did not deviate from that direction. Luckily, around noontime, I detected a shining spot in the distance. I stood still with a smile on my face. It must be a brook or a stream!

I also noticed that the ground on which I was walking was slowly rising, and that the brook or stream must be descending from a higher spot. I stopped, placed my knapsack on the ground, and surveyed the space that enfolded me. The vague range of the mountains that stood before my eyes as I was walking northward now appeared to me rather distinctly. I examined its topology to see if a mountain, or more than one, could be distinguished, but I did not recognize anything that could be identified as such. I remained in my position for a few minutes, trying again and again to see whether I missed the slope of a mountain, but to no avail.

Before consulting the compass about my next route, I went to that shiny spot. It was a stream. The water was clear as crystal. I quenched my thirst, filled my canteen, and then took a bath in it. A breath of life streamed through my heart and mind. I felt refreshed, renewed. I examined both banks of the stream to see if any vegetation thrived there and was able to identify a patch of cabbage. I uprooted one, smelled it, and then tasted it. It was safe. I picked two more and washed them in the clean stream. The instinct of survival was gradually asserting itself in my consciousness; I followed the wisdom implicit in it. There was room for the cabbage in my knapsack.

Although I was unable to identify the peakless mountain or any other mountain, I decided to march northward. This was the direction everyone should take to reach the peakless mountain. Nevertheless, doubt began to creep into my mind when I suddenly felt that the terrain was rising, and that the mountain range was closer than I had thought it was. The range was now standing before my eyes as a series of mountain ridges. There was no sign or suggestion of a peakless mountain, though. I looked at the compass once more, only to ascertain that I was, indeed, still marching northward. The view that was waiting for me was rather vague, nebulous, because it was overgrown with big bushes, low-growing plants, and mounds. I surveyed it carefully. Not a hint of a peakless mountain!

Bewildered, I stood motionless in my place for several minutes, trying to determine the direction of my next move, but nothing about the landscape that surrounded me pointed the way. I took another look at the compass. Its hand pointed northward, and northward I decided to go! I did not have any qualms about my decision. But the walk was neither easy nor short because walking uphill is harder than walking downhill, and because the foot of the mountain range looked a bit distant. However, I was not intimidated by this realization. I simply plowed my way through the rough and rising terrain. On a number of occasions, I stopped to drink some water and rest a little. I was always on the lookout for fruit, edible plants, and running water. Twice I saw snakes slithering between the rocks and the dead bushes on both sides of my trail. I ignored them, and they ignored me. My main concern was to find my way through and over the rocks that stood on my path, which must have peeled off the side of the mountain ridge.

Fatigue had already settled into my muscles when the sun began to move toward the western side of the mountain range. It was time to find a shelter for the night. Because the hills and big bushes were becoming sparse and the rocks dominant, I found it necessary to look for a spot near a big rock or a cave-like formation. This type of shelter was within reach because the rocks were very many. Still, I needed some bushes to create an enclosure. While I was searching for them, I discovered blueberry vines. I hauled the bushes to the site of my shelter and went back for the blueberries. The shelter I chose was a rather narrow space between three rocks. I created a "hut" that was similar to the one I had created out of the notch the evening prior.

Water was my main concern when I resumed my trip the following morning. The basic ingredients that are indispensable for human survival such as rice, beans, salt, dry fruits and vegetables, and canned meat were still intact in my knapsack. As for water, I kept my eyes open for a brook or perhaps a spring that was flowing from the foot of the mountain range. But the main challenge I faced soon after I resumed my journey was the increasing density of the rocks. Some of them were extremely large; it was difficult to circumvent the huge ones, and it was more difficult to climb over them.

But with a sense of determination and patience, I managed to move onward, always consulting my compass to make sure that I was not straying from my northward trail. I had to stop several times only to rest and hydrate myself, because the sun was getting warmer and warmer. My main objective was to discover the way to the peakless mountain. This objective was transformed into a worry immediately after the sun moved closer to the western horizon. I needed water, and I needed to know how and when I would find a path to the peakless mountain! I did not succumb to my worry, though, and I did not allow it to infringe on my courage or determination move on.

Shortly after the sun sank behind the mountain range and peace spread over the terrain, I heard the sound of water running between the rocks to my left; it sounded like a small cataract. I stopped, put my knapsack on the ground, and ran toward it. Yes, a brook was tumbling through those rocks! I crouched and drank some of its water and then went back to my knapsack and fetched my canteen and a small towel. I filled the canteen and took a sponge bath. Feeling refreshed, I climbed over a large rock and scanned my surroundings in search of wild fruits and a place to spend the night. It was not difficult to secure such a place because the rocks were abundant, but finding fruits or vegetables was hard for the same reason. Nevertheless, I made a special effort to locate an area covered with bushes or trees.

That night's makeshift "hut" was not different from the one I built the night before, but it was chillier. This was to be expected; I was practically at the foot of the mountain range. But I was not a stranger to cold weather. I had spent several years at the University of Waterloo in northern Ontario, Canada, and the University of Connecticut. In fact, I developed a liking for the cold weather. Anyway, I woke up next morning revived and with a vigorous sense of enthusiasm.

"I must be close to the foot of the peakless mountain!" I mumbled as I wound my way through the rocks. Around noontime, I decided to climb a rock and take a look at what awaited me in the distance. I was astonished to notice that I was in the midst of a forest of rocks, and that this forest seemed to be connected with the mountain range. I scrutinized the scene carefully but with a feeling of anxiety. I pulled out the compass from my knapsack and followed its pointer northward. No nick or passageway of any kind was in sight. The mountain range stood before me as a solid, formidable wall.

The appearance of that wall aroused a feeling of pensiveness in my mind. Unawares, I felt that a knot forming on my forehead! "No," I whispered in the silence of my soul and the landscape around me, "neither my grandmother nor the sun lovers who paid a visit to the peakless mountain before me were wrong about the existence of this mountain."

I looked again at the pointer of the compass and then marched onward, slithering my way through a forest of rocks. I was determined to reach its outer rim. I stood at a rather high rock when the sun was departing our Earth and cast an investigative look at the scene that surrounded me. My target was not its scientific composition, configuration, or aesthetic significance but a possible clue that might point the way to the peakless mountain. I lingered on the rock for a while and directed my attention to the foot of the ridge that stood before me as a solid wall. Disappointed, I could not detect any natural or human clue.

Nevertheless, I did not and could not give up. I descended the rock and proceeded toward the patch of land that separated the forest of rocks from the mountain ridge and, with my rucksack on my back, I walked alongside it, this time inspecting every part of my environs. Again, nothing suggested a clue that pointed the way to my mountain. I pulled out the compass from my rucksack and once more checked my direction. To my surprise, the hand pointed directly to the mountain where I was standing. "The clue must be around here!" I said involuntarily. Rather frantically, I walked toward a bulge a few feet from where I was standing. Lo and behold! The eastern side of that bulge shielded a fairly wide opening, wide enough for me to go through it without any difficulty. In truth, I did not hesitate to go through it.

The scene that was waiting for my eyes was extraordinary, mystifying. I had never encountered anything like it in the novels I read, in the movies I saw, and in all the stories my grandmother used to tell me when I was a young boy. A high mountain, whose peak eluded my vision because dusk had already made its way into that part of the mountain range, stood about one hundred meters away from me. The lower part of this mountain, which I was able to see, was densely covered with large, dark grey, shiny rocks, as if its form was designed by a cubist artist—as if the artist had been sitting at the crate of a violent volcano when she was designing it. The scene I saw was awesome, dreadful, beautiful, and mysterious. It was hard for me to contemplate this mountain, or the part I was able to embrace with my vision, without capitulating to its beauty and sublimity—to a triumphant dance between the beautiful and the sublime under the infinity of the sky that hugged the mountain and everything around me—and it was equally hard for me to miss the aura of the mystery that was oozing from within those rocks.

I do not recall how long I remained captive to that majestic spectacle, but I recall emerging from it with a feeling of amazement, humility, and a renewed passion to have an encounter with the sun. The feelings of fear, confusion, and fatigue that had been buzzing in my mind a few minutes ago vanished. I did not have a *eureka* experience similar to the one Archimedes had, but I did have a moment of deep contentment, of renewed faith in my mission. With a soft smile on my lips, I proceeded to inspect my environs.

A brook was flowing from the foot of that mountain; it was slithering its way through the rocks melodically. I enjoyed listening to it for a few minutes. "Was it singing a hymn to the mountain or perhaps to its author?" I wondered. "Why not? Who would not sing and dance to the mere mention of that author? Is his name not a ray of his presence?" Even though I did not recognize, I knew, without a shred of doubt, that it was the peakless mountain.

"You will recognize it when you see it. No one can miss it." My grandmother said in a whisper when she was on her death bed." Although it was not an integral part of the mountain range, it looked like a bas-relief rising from its bosom, asserting its independence on the one hand, and on the other, belonging to the range by emerging from it.

It was difficult to dwell for a long time on that challenging, exciting discovery; the sun that was illuminating the mountain range began to withdraw its final rays from that corner of the Earth. Without losing any time, I located a space similar to the one I has transformed it into a "hut" the night before, placed my knapsack in it, and gathered some leafy branches and bushes, not only to protect myself against the wind and possibly dangerous animals but also against the dampness and coolness that was typical of the Great Smokey Mountains. I searched for plant life, but unfortunately, I did not stumble on any plants or animals.

The terrain on which the mountain sat was simply rocky. A little anxious, but not worried, I went to the melodious brook and walked alongside its banks, hoping to find some kind of life on its shores. I did not find any. The idea of prospecting for fish crossed my mind. I pursued this idea and looked for a tarn. Luckily, I found two. I detected some fish in one of them. A smile flew from my mouth involuntarily. Devising a way to catch a few of them was a serious challenge for me because I had never fished. So, using my logical mind, I studied the design of the tarn and concluded that the best way to catch some of the fish was to block the entry of the water and trap them.

So, I gathered a few stones and blocked the fish from leaving the small tarn and then chased them with my hand. They outmaneuvered me several times and defiantly secured their freedom. But I did not give up. I garnered a few small stones and used them as a kind of dam. This trick was useful because I was able to corner a few fish and catch them. It is strange but satisfying to know the extent to which human mind can be resourceful in times of need, and how creative it can be when the challenges we face center on our survival! I built a small fire and cooked the fish. I ate two and saved the rest for the following day.

Dusk in that valley, which should be named Valley of The Sun, was pitch-dark. The fire I built to broil the fish lit my surroundings and warmed my "hut," but not for long, because very soon, the chill of the night seeped through the leafy branches and bushes of my hut and into my bones. I wore my woolen beanie, which I always wore during the night in wintertime, and I kept my jacket on when I crawled into my sleeping bag. It had been my habit to meditate before falling asleep every evening, but the chill of that evening froze my desire and with it my ideas to meditate. I struggled to fall asleep.

The golden rays of the sun were slowly mitigating the chill of the night and changing it into a soft mild warmth when dawn advanced into that region of the mountain range. The first task I performed was to go back to the tarn and catch a few more fish, which I cooked and saved for the following days. Then, I turned my attention to the next step of my journey: to determine the best way to ascend the peakless mountain. How could I or anyone climb a peakless mountain—one studded with cubical, hexagonal, octagonal, and multidimensional rocks—without a climbing gear? Alas! What was I expecting when I planned my trip? How knowledgeable was I about mountain climbing when I drew my plan? Did I plan it adequately? How can a soldier go to battle without weapons or skill in fighting? How can a teacher teach if she does not know *how* and *what* to teach? These questions were constant visitors of my mind, especially when the challenges of securing the means of my survival faced me.

The more I contemplated that mountain, the more I felt the depth of my naiveite and foolishness, not concerning the wisdom of seeking an audience with the sun but with my method of realizing it. I was so convinced, so passionate about the wisdom of having an audience with the sun that no power in the universe, no hardship, and no misfortune could either prevent or deter me from pursuing my goal. The question I confronted, and which was a source of anxiety, was the feasibility of my plan. Now, reflecting on my hastiness and naiveite makes me feel amazed, even guilty, at my naivete.

I did not doubt or desist from my pursuit. I examined the configuration of the rocks that made up the base of the mountain and began my ascent, moving between the rocks, not over them. My foot got stuck between those rocks several times, but with patience and skill I developed gradually, I climbed about two hundred feet over the course of the morning hours. I took at least three breaks, during which I rested and drank some water. The afternoon climb was more arduous and more challenging. I slid twice and bruised my chin. It bled a little, but I was able to medicate it and seal it with a Band-Aid. Later, one of my feet got stranded in a rather narrow chink formed by two adjoining rocks and was almost lost. Luckily, I was able to extricate it without incurring any harm.

Finding my way upward through the rocks was a daunting challenge—a real struggle. I do not know how I mustered the needed strength to face that challenge, but I did. More than once, Master Doubt appeared on the fringe of my consciousness with a comical smirk on his lips. At first, he did not say a word, but later on, he asked, "Where are you going? Are you going to meet the sun of all suns?" He let out a sarcastic chuckle and then added, "How? You can hardly gaze into the Earthly sun. How can you recognize, much less gaze into this all-encompassing sun?" Master Doubt continued: "Are you a fool? You must be! Show me an idealist who was able to realize his goal, and I show you the Garden of Eden. Ideals and lofty goals are noble visions. They exist in the minds of dreamers and nowhere else. The question is not having such visions, for the human imagination can easily create them, but attaining them. Neither the material nor the human world is hospitable or ready for such visions. Do not delude yourself—be true to your real self, the self that can thrive in this world, not in some imaginary world! At least, be realistic about what you can and cannot do."

I listened to this disrupter of human peace and reflected on the wisdom of his message, if it had any, but ignored it. "Neither this nor any other type of voice will dissuade me from my pursuit!" I thought, and I *felt what I thought.*

Just before the sun's rays were about to tilt to the western side of the sky, I had the surprise, indeed thrill, of my life. I stumbled on a clearing. I limped my way toward it and sat on its eastern side with my back against a rock. I sat on that side because I wanted to have a sun bath. A few minutes later, when I was able to breathe normally, I inspected the clearing because I was hoping, perhaps wishing, to discover my location in relation to the mountain and its surroundings. Proceeding slowly to the eastern side, because my foot was still hurting, I looked upward. The side of the mountain I was seeking was endless, or so it seemed, because the higher it rose, the more indistinct it became. It was impossible to detect a peak or anything else that might suggest one.

"Yes, it is the peakless mountain!" I mused as I moved around the clearing again. But this musing was transmuted into a reality when my eyes suddenly noticed a small, empty box on the edge of the clearing. I picked it up and examined it. It was a raisins box. A feeling of pleasure surged into my heart.

"I am not alone," I thought, "my fellow sun lovers were here. Like me, they took a break in this clearing." Fortified by this mysterious feeling of solidarity, I rested for almost one hour, only because the acute pain in my foot had not yet subsided. Water was uppermost on my mind.

"There must be a spring somewhere!" I murmured as I moved upward.

I encountered more than one clearing as I continued my climb, and I rested a little in each one of them. I always kept a vigilant eye for plant and animal life and especially for a spring a or a stream winding its way through the rocks. I was convinced that water could be found because patches of thick clouds were always passing over my head. It might seem strange, dear reader, if I observe that spending some time alone on a high mountain, in a desert, in the midst of a sea, or even in the midst of a crowd impels you to revaluate your sense of value and consequently to change your list of priorities, if you happen to have one.

On the precipice of the peakless mountain, I realized that the need for survival was my top priority, because it was a necessary condition for the attainment of my goal: I could not have an audience with the sun if I were dead! Almost instinctively, I found myself watching for plants, animals, and water. Fortunately, this need was met with a greater measure of success the higher I ascended the mountain; the density of the rocks was diminishing, and the probability of coming upon water and plants was increasing.

Shortly before I resumed my trip the following morning, I spotted a brook on the side of a huge boulder surrounded a large spread of smaller rocks. My immediate impulse was to take a sponge bath and fill my canteen with water. I sat on the bank of the brook for a little while and inspected the clearing in search of plant life. The area was barren. A flood of ideas and emotions zoomed into my mind. Although I was clear about my objective, I was in the dark about the road that led to it. Sitting, standing, or leaning your back against the wall of a rock in the dark can be confounding and sometimes enervating; it is like going everywhere but nowhere. Worse still, it can easily invite Master Doubt into your mind the way it did at that moment.

"But, no," I said to myself, "I am not in the dark; I am on the peakless mountain, and I am going to have an audience with the true sun."

But Master Doubt, who must have been listening to my monologue, whispered, "How?" This retort was not a test, I thought, because I was already on the mountain that led to my destination. "Are you sure?" Master Doubt asked sarcastically.

"I am!" I affirmed, and I proceeded into my ascent without hesitation. During a short respite I took a little later, when I was trying to find the best way to proceed, I inadvertently looked down toward the foot of the mountain, which seemed rather deep. I focused my attention on a large rock close to the bottom of the valley. To my surprise, I detected a rucksack and a number of objects strewn around it. I was startled. Curiosity propelled me to see whether a body was among those objects. There was none. I examined the area a few times only to ascertain the veracity of what I saw. I was not mistaken. It was a rucksack and human belongings, but a human body was not among them.

The startle that had found its way into my mind did not leave me; on the contrary, it seemed to settle there, and although it did not leave me entirely, it soon receded to the rim of my consciousness, as if Master Doubt intended it to be a constant reminder throughout my journey that he would not leave me alone! I stood frozen in my place and thought about the wisdom, perhaps folly, Master Doubt tried to stir in my mind. I was more inclined to reject his wisdom and more willing to endorse its folly, for I was certain that he understood the truth of human existence in reverse. With a somber state of mind, I went back to the brook and drank more of its water. I listened to its murmuring music as it was flowing down the mountain, carefree, rhythmic, and confident. Have you listened to the rhythm of nature in the rhythm of the cosmic process in the infinity of its details? If you have not, please, try! You will not regret the adventure.

I did not have time to reflect on the rucksack, on the objects strewn around it, or on the destiny of its owner because I had a long way to traverse that day. I followed the outline of the brook as it spiraled its way upward, but I did not do so for long, because it gradually vanished into the narrow spaces and slits formed by the rocks. Although the terrain was less rocky as I moved upward, it was more difficult to tread through it. It was getting steeper every few hundred feet. I soon learned that in this kind of terrain, one must walk slowly, conscientiously. The probability of rolling downhill was high, especially when you were carrying a knapsack. Nevertheless, I did not waver from my quest for the true sun. Neither the small, sometimes sharply edged stones that covered the ground on which I was walking, nor the image of the rucksack in that deep valley deterred me from my pursuit. I simply moved upward without looking backward. The moment I noticed that the sun was nearing the mountain range, I decided to look for a place to spend the night. Besides, it was time to nurse my bruised chin.

As soon as I arrived at a somewhat large clearing, I began looking for a brook and fruit-bearing plants. Although I was hopeful about finding water, I was not very optimistic about finding a brook, because brooks do not flow at very high elevation. I was almost certain, however, that I would find a spring, mainly because the caravans of thick clouds never stopped passing over the mountain range.

"But then," I wondered, "how can I find a spring, even if that is possible?"

The first thing I did was to place my knapsack near an agglomeration of rocks where I could create a shelter, and then I proceeded toward the boulders on the western side of the mountain. I moved slowly around it with an eye on plants and water to no avail. It might seem odd if I say that a few minutes into my search, I discovered a spring by means of my ears, not my eyes. I was examining a patch of big boulders when I heard the sound of water tumbling rhythmically among the boulders. But those rocks were large, igneous, smooth, and shiny on all sides. I inspected the spaces between them in order to identify the passage of the water. But contrary to my expectation, the assortment of the boulders I inspected was only the upper part of a large expanse of boulders that stretched deeply downhill. It was, at first, difficult to reach the site of the running water because the rocks were not level and were tilted downhill. If I was not extremely careful, I could have easily slid all the way to the valley to never see the light of day again.

After a comprehensive inspection of the configuration of the boulders, I was able to discover a safe way to reach the water. I took off my boots, hatched my canteen to my belt, stuck a small towel to my waist, and slowly moved to the smaller boulder, gliding over it like a snake toward the adjoining boulders and the running water, hanging onto the edge with my hands. I slid down more than once, but luckily, I was able to reach a wide opening. Softly, I dismounted the boulder and jumped to the ground. The spring had dug a rather narrow bed. I sat next to it, satiated a nagging thirst, took a sponge bath, filled the canteen, and cleaned the wound on my chin. I looked for plants or some sign of life. The area was almost barren. I sat next to the running water and lost myself to a short reverie. It is difficult for anyone to indulge in any kind of serious contemplation on this kind of journey, although sometimes one cannot help it, simply because the novelty of the natural scenes, the surprises you face, and because the urgent need to secure means of living dominates your consciousness most of the time.

One of the questions on my mind during that reverie was the extent to which I would find water, and how far I would climb toward the higher slopes of the mountain before the true sun allowed me an audience.

"How do you know that he will allow you an audience?" Master Doubt, who was following my train of thought, suddenly whispered in my left ear.

"I am certain he will!" I responded impulsively.

"Be logical, Mr. Philosopher! How can the infinite, the infinite that transcends every shape, substance, or kind of being, meet you on this desolate mountain?"

"You seem to forget that I am the seeker, and I am the one who should find a way to meet him."

"Where? How?" Master Doubt said sarcastically. "In what cranny, on what boulder, in what "hut," in what clearing, on what slope will you meet him? Just tell me, if you can! You are the most shallow, impractical, unimaginative philosopher I have ever met!"

"You speak as if you know the ways of the infinite. Do you know its ways?" Master Doubt grumbled and then fell silent.

I could not stop, so I added, "Do you know the infinite? How can you know the ways of any being if you do not know that being?" I knew that he heard me even though he did not answer my questions.

The fish I caught and cooked and the berry fruits I picked a few days ago were already depleted when I charged into my fourth day of ascending the peakless mountain. The pressing need to supplement the groceries I packed in my rucksack loomed at the front of my consciousness, and I felt the urgency of this need when I suddenly realized that my trip would be longer than I had expected. The mountain was, after all, peakless. Master Doubt's words fluttered in my ear. Where, when, and how would I meet my true sun? An answer to these questions was neither clear nor forthcoming. Not very soon, it seemed. I felt this urgency more acutely when, on the following day, I noticed that the mountain was becoming steeper and steeper, and that signs of life and water were becoming fewer and fewer. So, I decided to ration the remainder of the food in my knapsack and to be more attentive to possible sources of plants and water. But I did not let this new realization delay me from the pursuit of my goal. Everything in my life paled into insignificance compared to it!

On the fifth day, my climb was harder and slower than ever. The boulders were becoming sparser and the terrain steeper. I had to take four breaks in the morning that day. On more than one occasion, I looked downhill to see the foot of the mountain, but it was hardly visible. The foot that was rather clear to my vision two days ago was becoming a bottomless pit! I felt like I was standing in midair between two endless ends. Have you had this kind of experience, dear reader? What does it feel like to be in a state of floating, uprootedness, or without a tether? Do you know that in such a state, you develop, or perhaps acquire, a new sense of time, of space, and of place? Not only in relation to this or that point in the natural world but also in relation to your inner world and your social world. You see these worlds more clearly, in their transience and cosmic insignificance.

Water and a place to spend the night were my main focus when I felt the heat of the sun assaulting my body that afternoon. The heat was scorching hot! It penetrated my hat into my skull. I looked for a shaded area. There was none. The idea of spilling some water on my head flashed through my mind, but I declined it because water was becoming increasingly scarce. I even entertained the idea of saving some of my urine if the worst came to the worst. Nevertheless, I pressed on, always seeking the shortest route upward.

I felt somewhat better when the sun began to sink behind its western horizon, for this meant that the heat would sink with it. However, this happy prospect did not last long because I suddenly slid, and losing my balance, I swayed to the left a little and then tumbled downhill. Luckily, my descent into the valley of my extinction was obstructed by a small boulder. It took me a few seconds to recover my consciousness. My eyes were facing the ascending side of the mountain when I regained it. Fear of making the wrong move, especially of sliding further downward, prevented me from moving my body. Rolling downhill with a knapsack on can be injurious, if not fatal. I needed to make sure that my legs and arms were intact, because my mission, and possibly my life, would be aborted without them.

I remained in that position until I was certain that I did not have any broken bones, and then I slowly rose to my feet and leaned my back against the boulder. This posture enabled me to adjust my knapsack to my back, and looking upwards, I cautiously ambled at a very slow pace. A few minutes later, I noticed that the ground on which I was standing was gravel; it was shifty! But neither the gravel nor the possibility of losing my life made a dent, not even a small one, in my determination to continue my trip.

It became almost customary on my ascent to keep a watchful eye for a tract of land somewhere in the distance. But that afternoon, my eyes were particularly watchful for a possible shelter. Rest was an urgent need. However, my next station was quite appropriate for physical, but not mental, rest. It looked like a park strip carved out as a cave in the mountain. I was both surprised and delighted to come upon this hollow space. But I was shocked, indeed frightened, out of my wits, when I ambulated toward its interior. A rucksack was placed on its southern side. A canteen was hanging on its side, but no one, not even a fly, was around.

"Hello!" I shouted, but no one responded to my call. Then I shouted again; no one answered. I waited a few moments and shouted again, and again, no one answered my call. Silence reigned over the space of that cave! Bewildered, I walked toward the edge of the strip and shouted "hello" again. Unfortunately, no one answered. There was no echo to my call; it must have been swallowed by the infinite space that enfolded the mountain. I moved closer to the edge to see if someone was around the strip. Alas, the moment I placed my foot on it the ground under it crumbled and splintered into a heap of sand. I rolled down the slope in the direction of the bottomless pit. My right foot flew into the air, and I was about to slide down with the heap of sand. But, to my good fortune, I was able to place my arms on the two sides of the hole created by my slide and hold on to them with all the strength I could muster.

I pushed my back with the speed of light. The crumbling process stopped. Slowly, very slowly, I pushed my body backward, relying on my elbows and not allowing my feet to touch the sand. I kept pushing my body like this until I felt like I was in a safe zone. With fear buzzing in my mind and heart, I practically tiptoed my way to the strip and along its side, testing the ground not in order to walk on it but to see whether or not it was firm. It was soft in a few places but firm alongside the edge. I surveyed the area with the eyes of an eagle to locate my fellow sun lover or his body, but I could not, because that side of the maintain was very steep. I repeated the survey a few times, to no avail. Downhearted, I went back to the two knapsacks and placed them in the corner of the cave where I planned to spend the night.

Unlike my previous adventures, that one was not very hard because there were not many boulders around the strip. But moving around and between them was not easy. Although my search for water and life was fruitless, I did not give up. I mounted one of the boulders and scanned the surrounding area to see if I could spot running water, but no water or signs of life were in sight. I demounted the boulder and mounted another. Again, no water and no life were in sight. Nevertheless, I was reluctant to give up. No person in her right mind would, I think, give up in such a moment.

"There must be some water around here! There are clouds, therefore, there must be water!" I caught myself murmuring.

I climbed another boulder. And yes, there was water; I discovered it alongside the boulder on the lowest stretch of the precipice. I maneuvered my way to that spot. Water was flowing from a spring on its northern side. But I was unable to feel pleased about my discovery, however, because the sadness that had filled my heart would not leave it.

The sense of adventure disappeared the moment I demounted the boulder and proceeded to my shelter; it was replaced by a sense of presentiment intermixed with a feeling of sorrow for the death of my fellow sun lover.

"Did he suffer? Did he die with a feeling of regret, perhaps frustration? Did he want or expect anyone to mourn him after his death? How can a seeker of the sun die or suffer? How can a spark illuminated by the light of the ultimate sun fade away?" These and other questions were the object of my attention when I reached the "hut." But these questions, and my soul with them, stopped before the knapsacks that were waiting for me.

"Oh no," I thought. I did not see his knapsack, or even mine. I saw the image of my fellow sun lover waiting for me. His face, and especially his eyes, looked like the face and the eyes of the people who descended into Hades the way Homer described them long time ago. His complexion was pale, pale as Hades itself! I gazed into his eyes for a few seconds and mumbled a frightened greeting, but he did not respond to me. My greeting flew from my lips involuntarily, unconsciously. Oh, goodness! What force prompted this greeting to fly from my lips? Well, it did, and I could not help it. The apparition simply stared at me with two blank eyes. Even though I knew he was dead, still, I wished I could speak to him. Those eyes must have felt my wish because he shook his head negatively, as if to say, "No, do not try!"

"Can I ask—?" I staggered.

"Do not ask!"

"One—only one question?" The pale resumed its stare. "Continue?" I asked.

"To the death!" the pale face said and vanished.

I could not believe that this conversation had actually taken place, but it must have, at least in my head.

"But are you sure?" Master Doubt whispered in my left ear.

"Yes!" I mumbled.

That was an apparition, and the conversation was a concoction of my imagination. Was I speaking to myself? Was I expressing, or perhaps justifying, my own doubts and fears about the reasonableness of my mission? Or could it be that Master Doubt was trying to test me again? The mere entertainment of these questions sent a shudder into my mind. This shudder opened my eyes to the tasks I should perform and the possible dangers I might be facing in the coming days.

With a melancholy state of mind, I prepared my evening meal and ate it in reverent silence. I was reluctant to touch my fellow sun lover's rucksack that evening. His absence was present in the cave and with me. The human in us exists in space and time, but it is omnipresent in every heart that is illuminated by the light of the divine spark in our hearts.

It was hard to meditate about any question or idea that evening, especially because I was mourning for my friend, the friend I never had the privilege to meet. It is sacrilegious to allow any feeling or thought into your mind when your heart is grieving for the death of a friend. Living the sadness of his or her loss is the most appropriate way to grieve for her, to honor her.

Morpheus embraced me tightly with his warm arms that night.

Chapter Six

God Speaks

T HE first object I noticed when I opened my eyes to the world on the
following morning was my friend's rucksack. It was sitting next to
mine the way I left it the night before. I cast a long look at both rucksacks
in solemn silence. Why did he have to miss his audience with the sun?
Why did he die on this kind of mission? Lack of faith? No, because he recommended that I continue my mission to the death. How could he have
delivered this recommendation if he had not been a genuine believer? If he
had not been craving union with god? Goodness! Why should good causes,
genuine human beings, and lovers of the sun die immaturely? Why should
innocence be crushed by the ruthless hand of the irrational?

Recalcitrant questions concerning the meaning of human life—of
love, death, and life—questions we cannot answer, do not usually leave us.
Rather, they recede into some corner of our minds and wait there until they
are summoned by a new quandary, adversity, or an unexpected surprise we
face in the course of our lives. These questions are not fortuitous or trivial;
they are responses to essential demands of human nature. It is extremely
difficulty for one to be human without asking them, and it is difficult for
the person who asks them to not desire answers to them. Could I remain
silent when a fellow seeker of the true sun died an untimely death alone on
the peakless mountain? I could not! I was sad, and I wanted to know why
he had died such a death.

And yet, I could not linger for a long time on these questions, not
at that critical juncture of my journey, because the rays of the sun were
actively illuminating the mountain range. I emptied my friend's rucksack
and inspected its contents. They were similar to mine. I squeezed them into

my knapsack and clipped his canteen to the other side of my waist before leaving the cave.

The mountain was getting slimmer, steeper, and lonelier the higher I ascended. It was my practice to look upward, not downward, when I was climbing. But around noon that day, I felt an itch to look downward to see how far I had travelled. I did, but there was no bottom, and no point of reference that enabled me to know where I was or how far I had ascended. There was depth—pure depth. No matter how long you look at pure depth in search of some object or form you can use as a point of reference, you see nothing.

Then I looked upward. There was no peak, no top of any kind. There was depth—pure depth. The only thing my eyes could see was the stretch of the mountain on which I was gradually walking, disappearing into that depth. This recognition was a bit perturbing, but this perturbation vanished when I proceeded into my ascent. It is always important to know where we are. But how can we know where we are or where we are going without a point of reference? At that point, my only point of reference was my goal, and I felt that I was approaching it. I knew it existed, and I knew I should realize this on the peakless mountain. This knowledge was the source of my hope, courage, and faith.

The higher I ascended, the slower my ascent was. I had to rest often because the ground was becoming increasingly shifty, and I had to develop a strategy to prevent myself from sliding downhill. But I soon discovered that, although it was effective most of the time, this strategy was not effective all the time because I slid downhill more than once. One time, the slide, which seemed unstoppable, given that I was rolling downward like an avalanche, was to my good fortune obstructed by a patch of bushes. I crawled upward on the trench that my downward slide had dug and then continued my ascent diligently, looking for a boulder, a precipice, or some other kind of ledge. That incident was an eye-opener, perhaps a warning that I should learn how to step on soft ground.

The storm of fear that whirled into my mind a few minutes ago did not leave me; on the contrary, it found its way into every fiber of my being. I could not help but recreate the image of my slide. When an event is so scary and/or life-threatening, it grips us and digs a place for itself in the subconscious. But although it was an image, the mere thought of the scene made me cringe with fright. The notion of my extinction hovered on the fringe of my consciousness. Have you ever imagined or even thought of your non-existence, dear reader? Have you tried to imagine your extinction without leaving a trace, or some kind of significant memory or accomplishment, in this world? Or, have you tried to imagine the non-existence of your accomplishments in this world, as if you had never existed in it—of the critical moments of pain, pleasure, failure, success, creation, or struggle in your pursuit of what you deemed truly important?

Yes, on that mountain, I imagined the stream of significant moments that made up the thread of my life and watched it the way you watch a movie. I also imagined its sudden transition into oblivion. My heart sank into my belly. I shivered. I felt what a soldier feels when the doctor amputates his leg, and I felt what any rational being would feel when his life is amputated from the realm of existence! I did not only think, I also *felt* what it means for human life to be dear. I did not wish it to disappear, at least not before I met the true sun! But the mountain I was ascending was becoming increasingly tortuous, increasingly hard to climb. A stiff frown spread over my forehead, and the pale face of my fellow sun lover loomed before my eyes. "To the death!" This response rang loudly and clearly in mind and in my ear! My fellow sun lover meant to say, "Fill your mind with courage and yes, with faith!"

The apparition vanished, but not the wisdom and certainly not the spirit of love that radiated from it.

"Neither struggle, nor pain, nor death can quench my passion for the true sun!" I whispered as I continued my ascent. I encountered several clusters, and sometimes jumbles of boulders where I rested, but none afforded an appropriate shelter for the night. Nonetheless, I pressed on despite the advent of the dark. Although I was indifferent to the hunger that was itching my stomach, I could not be indifferent to the chill that had begun to sweep into my flesh. I stopped and removed a light jacket, which had belonged to my late fellow sun lover, and wore it. I was certain that he would have wanted me to wear his jacket and also eat the food he packed in his rucksack.

Dusk was spreading its wings on the mountain when I spotted a heap of boulders in the distance. Its appearance fired an arrow of enthusiasm into my mind. I proceeded toward it at a faster but extremely careful pace. Because the wind was blowing from the east, I looked for a possible enclosure on the western side. It was easier to find a notch, but it was harder to find bushes that would function as a roof. In fact, it was practically dark when I discovered some small patches of bushes, and by then, it was almost impossible to look for a spring or vegetation. Nevertheless, I built a "hut" and ate a reasonably wholesome meal, but I was not able to reflect on the extraordinary happenings of the day. Both my body and my mind involuntarily submitted to an urgently needed seep.

To my surprise, on the following morning, I did not wake up to the golden rays of the sun as I had throughout my journey. In truth, it was not a morning at all, although I had a restful sleep, because the whole mountain around me was enfolded by a thick spread of fog. It was difficult to see any object in the vicinity. For a moment, I felt that I was in a prison cell. I looked at my watch; it was nine o'clock. I gathered the bushes that made up the roof of my "hut" into a pile and set it on fire. The heat gave me some warmth and dispelled the fog from my immediate surroundings.

Soon after I ate my morning meal, I sat next to the fire and waited for the passage of the fog, but the wait was not idle; it gave me an occasion to evaluate my ascent and the conditions under which I might encounter the true sun. A bundle of the questions that had been waiting for answers moved from the inner folds of my mind to the front.

"How can a finite being like you, a being who is no more than a speck, seek an encounter with the infinite? How can a sun, which is no more than a flicker in the universe, have an audience with the sun of all suns? Suppose an audience is possible; what kind of audience will, or can, it be? What will happen during it? Have you been wise in seeking such an audience, or was it an expression of a narcissist ego? You are ascending the peakless mountain—how far do you plan or expect to ascend? How long can you travel on this *endless trail*? What makes you think that its higher elevations will be hospitable to a frail creature like you? What makes you think that your fate will be different from the fate of your fellow sun lover?"

These questions, which had visited me on many different occasions in the past several days, were released from the chains of my subconscious by Master Doubt, or perhaps by the caring hand of wisdom. Regardless of who instigated them, they made sense. I really think that no seeker of the infinite could have ignored them.

It is always important to know where you are with respect to what you are doing, be it in your family, profession, social life, or with respect to your life-project, in order to avoid the possibility of *drifting* in your life. One's goal in life is her ultimate anchor—her point of reference.

At that moment of my journey, I was one with my goal, and my goal was an audience with the true sun. I was certain that the trail I was following should lead to it. I was also certain that it was the worthiest goal any human being could seek. This knowledge was a rich source of courage and faith in what I was doing. Master Doubt had a right to question my resolve and faith in pursuing my goal to the very end, regardless of the hardships I might face! I did not deny the difficulty of realizing my goal, and I was ready to die for it. I felt that I would not be true to myself if I did not meet the true sun—not according to my wishes and expectations, but according to the truth implicit in its light. Even though I did not fully know this truth, I was certain that I would recognize it when I encountered it. Truth does not hide and cannot be veiled, at least not for long or forever, because its essence is a radiance of the true sun.

My ascent that day was demanding because the terrain was getting steeper, the terrain rougher, and the climate colder. Looking for a source of water was my priority that morning, for I could not continue my ascent without it. I stopped and inspected every heap of rocks, every cliff, and every trench I stumbled upon. This search did not come to an end until noontime. My chest heaved heavily but slowly when I filled my canteens with water and then quenched my thirsty stomach. Refreshed, I proceeded into my ascent with a greater measure of enthusiasm and hope but only for a short time. I suddenly found myself stranded on a plateau that was surrounded by very steep elevation. Almost all of the sides of this elevation were soft, so that the moment I stepped on any part of it, it crumbled and splintered into fine gravel. I moved around this plateau and tried to climb a few times, to no avail.

"Impossible!" I mumbled. "There must be a way to go over this strip!"

I pulled out a small pickax the size of a hammer from my knapsack and dug a small trench in the strip. That was an onerous task because the ground was soft, but I was able to overcome that obstacle and move on.

Over the next three days, which were not different from the previous days, I frequently reflected on the last station of my trip. Two questions figured prominently in this reflation: "Where?" and "When?" I was preoccupied with them, not because I was wavering in the wisdom of my mission but because the ascent was becoming increasingly stubborn. Contrary to the human spirit, the body has its limits, and these limits cannot be ignored. I felt those limits, but I did not allow myself to be constricted by them. I pressed onward.

"Neither my body, nor the chill of the air, nor the ruggedness of the terrain will deter my me from my pursuit!" I thought, as I always did when the consciousness of a challenge stared me in the face. I was as stubborn in my determination as the terrain was in its ascent. I speak of the limits of the human body only because I discovered them in their true nature on that ascent, and I mention them in this context only to accentuate the need for genuine understanding, passion, and faith in the validity of one's mission. Please, dear reader, do not underestimate the power of human passion and faith in human life. Can the scientist, the philosopher, the artist, or the social reformer shatter the wall of the routine, the ordinary, and open up the door of the creative impulse without faith and passion in the goal she seeks?

When I opened my eyes to the light of the sun on the twelfth day of my ascent, I stood at the door of my "hut" and gazed into the blue sky: "When?" "Where?" These two questions rang their bell again into my ear. I knew there was going to be a where and a when, but I was desirous to know the answer to my questions. That desire sprang from my passion for the true sun and nothing else, and my passion grew in intensity the higher I ascended. Does your longing for your beloved, who has been away for a while, not grow in intensity when you recognize that the time of her arrival is drawing nearer and nearer?

I cannot say whether it was caused by mental distraction, a sudden surge of zeal, or fatigue, but I inadvertently fell to the ground and slid down the mountain with my knapsack attached to my shoulders and my canteens to my waist. It was impossible for me to stop the slide because there were no boulders or bushes to obstruct it. My body must have rolled down quite a distance, as I discovered later on. It was equally impossible to determine how long I had rolled down that slippery side of the mountain, and it was equally impossible to know how I survived that most dangerous slide, for I was unconscious of my body and my surroundings during that fall. But I remember regaining my consciousness in a cave that was suffused with an angry storm of thunder and a fierce wind blustering its way through that storm. Every wall and space of that cave was quaking and trembling.

This frightful spectacle choked every vital power of my mind. I was so frightened, I was quaking and trembling with the quaking and tumbling of the cave! At that moment, I was unconscious of my body—whether it was bruised or whether any part of it was fractured or broken. I was not even conscious of whether I was in pain. All I remember is that I was captive to that spectacle. When the extraordinary and the extraordinarily frightful surpasses the power of your intellect, feelings, and imagination and stands before your eyes and ears in the fullness of its might, you cannot think, feel, or speak. You simply surrender yourself to its grip, to the destiny that hides within that grip.

But this spectacle exploded into a more remarkable, more frightful, more overpowering, and more exquisite scene because almost instantaneously, a marvelous flood of light, one I cannot describe, flowed from the bosom of that spectacle without silencing its thunder, halting the quakes, or calming the fierce wind in the cave. It seemed to me that the mightiest forces of the universe surged from the infinite depth of *being* and allowed that flood of light to shine into that cave. What can your eyes and ears do in the presence of such a flood of light? The only thing they can do, and what I did, was to stand in it in awe, in *absolute awe*.

At that moment, I was not trembling and quaking because I was afraid of what was happening in the cave and within me, for there was no room in my consciousness for any kind of feeling. I was quaking and trembling because the spectacle I was witnessing was, to speak plainly, remarkable in its grandeur, splendor, and magnificence. It was tremendous—the tremendous in itself. I trembled more frantically and squeaked involuntarily when a most voluminous voice burst from the depth of that flood of light the way lava bursts from an angry volcano.

"Why are you here?" the voice thundered. "Speak!"

But I could not speak. I did not know what to say, and I did not how to respond to such a thundering voice—at least not immediately. How could I or any human being, regardless of how wise, courageous, noble, or strong she might be, speak in the presence of such a spectacle and to such a voice? Please, let me correct myself: it was impossible to characterize what I was seeing and hearing or even to characterize the voice I was hearing as a *voice*. The voice surpassed the power of my mind—or any mind—to categorize it. What I am saying is that this is my only way of describing the experience I had in that cave to the best of my ability. Treat what I say as a series of metaphors. But I should remind you that sometimes, metaphors are more expressive than the concepts of the philosopher or the scientist.

Yes, it was really hard to respond to that voice because I had to collect my scattered self and transform it into a subject that could think and speak. That transformation was not an easy task, but I had no choice. Goodness! Who could have a choice in the presence of such a spectacle? And on the other hand, who could fail to collect herself in the presence of such a spectacle? Does such a spectacle not inspire the mind with the vision, strength, and skill required to stand on its feet and speak? It might seem strange to say that when I was ready to speak, my mind was swarming with ideas and questions.

I involuntarily blurted out, "You speak! Yes, you speak!"

"Of course I speak!"

"But how can you speak if your speech transcends, infinitely transcends, every possible kind of speech? Please, be patient with me—how can the unspeakable speak?"

"The unspeakable speaks *because* he is the unspeakable, *because he is the original* fountain *of all speech*, because he is the inexhaustible source of any and all imaginable form of expression, and most of all, because he is the fountain of all being."

"But," I said, "*how* can the unspeakable speak?"

There was a moment of silence and then a grumble. "Explain yourself."

"The unspeakable is the absolutely infinite, and because it is absolutely infinite, it is indescribable and therefore unspeakable. But in speaking to me or to anyone else, does he not become finite? How can the infinite become or appear in any finite mode of being? How can the *infinitely unspeakable speak finitely*?"

"It can, because *speech*, which you call *reason* and sometimes *conversation*, is an essential dimension of its being. Reason becomes conversation the moment it speaks. Thus, it exists as reason when it speaks. It becomes the reason it is and should be in the mode of conversation. Again, reason is reason only because it speaks. Otherwise, it is not reason. What it says when it speaks is an expression of its inner being. Its speech *flows* from its nature as reason. Accordingly, inasmuch as the universe is an emanation from the infinite *qua reason*, it expresses and necessarily reveals the rational nature of the infinite. The real is rational because it flows from infinite reason. How can you speak of the laws of nature or causation, without which neither philosophy nor physics is possible?"

"We can, then, view the universe and everything that exists as a cosmic conversation? I assume that this process is an emanation from the depth of the infinite."

"Yes, your inference is correct," the voice said.

"But then, how can the infinite source of conversation take place with a finite, lowly, being like me? Or, how can the infinite converse with a finite being?" I asked with trembling lips.

"It can! Do not insult your intelligence! If I am the infinite conversation, and I am, if I am the creative source of all being, and I am, if my creation emanates from my inner being, and it does, do you not think that I can communicate with a finite, lowly being like you? A being whose very existence and essence is an extension of my own conversation, of my own being? How many times in your lectures at Lambeth College have you argued before your students that the infinite is *immanent in its creation*? Does the parent in your world not converse with its infant, the teacher with its student, and the lover with her beloved?"

"I *understand* what you say, but I cannot *comprehend* what I understand? How can I comprehend the incomprehensible?" I said with the same trembling lips. "I understand the logic of what you say, but I cannot comprehend its connotation, its referent."

"How can you not comprehend it when you are conversing with me?"

"I am conversing with you, and I am reasoning validly, but do I comprehend my conversation with you, its author? How can I be said to comprehend my conversation with you *if I cannot comprehend you*? I know I am having this conversation with you, but I do not comprehend its signification. I believe, but I do not comprehend what I believe. You are the one I seek to comprehend!"

"Do you think that having this conversation is a basis for comprehending what you understand and believe?"

"I can understand what my mind thinks and imagines, but I cannot comprehend what transcends its powers of thinking and imagination. These two powers are appropriate for a finite being like me, but they are not appropriate for the infinite mind."

"Your modesty is commendable, but your thinking is flawed. If you can understand what I say, you can comprehend more, much more, than than what I say, otherwise, you would not have struggled all your adult life, and especially during the past twelve days. You would not be here in this place, and you would not be having this conversation with me now, if you did not also comprehend more than what you understand or what it means for me to be infinite. Understanding without comprehension can take place in the human mind as an abstract or conceptual activity.

"But such an activity is not exclusive of the mind, and it is not exclusive of abstract thinking, because ideas always point to what they signify—to their source, to what lies beyond them. They can be bridges that lead the mind to what lies beyond them. The mind of the metaphysician or the mystic is not interested in ideas but in their sources. Thus, when the mind moves from the level of abstract to existential thinking, from the level of *reasoning* to the level of *intuiting* their ground, it can be said to comprehend what it thinks. This type of comprehension usually, but not necessarily, takes place in meditation."

"But," I could not prevent myself from interrupting the voice, "how can I think of you or the infinite? For, even if I have an idea of the infinite, which is no more than a finite reality in my mind, even if I move in an event of meditation from the idea to its ground, I cannot comprehend this ground because its being transcends my powers of comprehension. Thinking the idea of the infinite is different from comprehending it in an act of intuition. How can I think it if I do not comprehend it?"

"But meditation on the idea, which points and necessarily leads to its signification, will enable you to stand on the edge that overlooks the infinite. Standing on that edge, as you have done, contemplating the boundlessness of the infinite—or the extent of being your mind can reach in this activity—will justify the claim that in discoursing on the infinite, you can comprehend what it thinks."

"But can it comprehend it in its infinite being?"

"It can comprehend it as infinite although it cannot comprehend it in the fullness of its being. This is why you can, as you are now doing, stand in *its presence*, feel it, and know what it means to be in the presence of the infinite."

"Its presence? How?"

"Standing in its presence is standing in the light of its effulgence, the kind of radiance that emanates from the depth of its infinity. Your longing to see me has been a longing to reach this edge; it has been a longing to stand in the radiance of its presence."

"Then, please, let me comprehend another aspect of your being."

"Go ahead!"

"I understand you when you say that conversation is an essential dimension of your being. Does this mean that you, yes you, the absolutely infinite, have spoken, and that it continues to speak in different languages?"

"If I am the original conversation, and I am, then I am the one who has been speaking to all the people of the world from the dawn of history to the present moment, and I shall continue to speak to them endlessly."

"And in different languages?"

"In one language—my language. There cannot be more than one language!"

"But how can one language be different languages at the same time? Now you are speaking English with me. But how can you speak Chinese, Aramaic, Russian, Italian, and other languages with others?"

"I speak by revealing myself to finite beings or any seekers of knowledge. *Revelation* is the language I speak."

"How? What is the structure of your language?"

"Light, the language I speak, is the medium by which I reveal myself; it reveals aspects of my being. Therefore, light speaks because what it reveals comes into being in and through light."

"How does light speak?"

"By being light."

"How does it reveal your nature or your will?"

"You have to learn to see the light, to penetrate deeply into its essence, into the infinity of the meaning implicit in it. Light does not argue, deceive, or hide itself. Do you not have to learn to see the meaning implicit in a work of art? Do you learn how to perceive meaning as a type of reality? Does the aesthetic object hide itself? It seems to be hidden only to those who cannot or do not want to perceive and feel meaning. Has it occurred to you that beauty, truth, and love are different modes of luminous presence? Have you ever entertained the idea that this luminosity is the essence of the spiritual dimension of the artwork?

"But now, I ask you to lift your eyes to a higher realm of meaning, to a realm that is infinite in its dimension and depth, to a realm that is the spring from which not only this or that meaning in this or that area pf human experience flows, but also the infinity of meaning that underlies the being of purpose and everything that exists or will ever exist."

"If you speak by revealing yourself, in what sense is revelation speech or speaking?"

"Any episode of revelation in which a human being aspires to converse with me and succeeds in standing in my presence is an event of conversation. In this event, the aspirant seeks to know something *about* me or *from* me. What she discovers about me or the message she receives from me is not delivered as a syntactical or symbolic form, be it linguistic, cultural, or artistic, but as a radiance of meaning, a meaning implicit in my essence. She articulates this meaning in a certain symbolic form that can be communicated in a particular cultural language and setting."

"When you speak of revelation," I said, "do you mean that in an encounter with an aspirant, or perhaps with one of your lovers, you disclose something hidden about yourself?"

"Hidden?" the voice rumbled. "There is nothing hidden about me. I do not hide anything about my nature or anything I do to anyone. I am revelation, *pure and simple*. I am the *ultimate radiance of infinite being*!"

"Then," I said, "how should we explain the different and frequently contradictory testimonies, understandings, descriptions, images, interpretations, symbols, and claims about you by the different philosophers, artists, religions, and mystics?"

"I am an inexhaustible source of meaning. The aspirant is a finite being. She might or might not succeed in capturing the radiance of my being adequately or even correctly. We should not complain about their deficiencies in the perception, understanding, or interpretation of the truth of my radiance. This type of deficiency is common among philosophers, religions, and artists. It is the source of much conflict, misunderstanding, and violence among individuals and communities, but it is not common among the wise philosophers, founders of most religions, and the truly imaginative artists."

"And how, then, should we explain the difference between them?" I asked.

"My way."

"Your way?" I retorted hastily. "What is your way?"

"Rational conversation."

"How?"

"As you should have already discovered, rational conversation is the royal road to the edge. All the disagreements, aporias, conflicts, and contradictions between the philosophers, theologians, and scientists, that divide people into parties and incline them to hate, fear, harm, and kill dissolve into clarity in the radiance of rational conversation. This light does not only illuminate the source of these disagreements, conflicts, contradictions, and aporias but also reconciles them in the bond of the truth of that radiance. This truth is the ultimate criterion by which any claim, principle, or law is evaluate and judged."

"As a derivative question," I said, "can we say that conversation is the high road to the creative act in general?"

"Creation?" the voice thundered with an obvious tone of dissatisfaction. This word is forbidden in my presence. You can use it metaphorically but not ontically. Human beings need metaphors; I do not."

"Why?"

"Because in its very essence, the creative act is a dialogical act: conversation is its medium, substance, and the power that makes it possible. You will not be amiss if you say that *reason* is the stuff and formative power of the creative act. The fabric of that which creates and that which is created is reason and nothing else. Does the artist create the paint, the line, the marble, the sound, the motion, or the word when she creates her artwork? Or does she create a spiritual world—one that is fashioned by the vision and magical power of reason?

"Next, is the act of artistic creation not a dialogue between the artist *qua reason* and herself, and on the one hand, the art world, human life, and nature? And is the activity of aesthetic perception not a dialogue between the work and the perceiver? Have you ever heard of an aesthetic object fortuitously jumping out of the artwork into the mind of the perceiver? Finally, have you heard of a medium acquiring a significant form, a form that embodies meaning?"

"But then, is the creative act an activity in which something comes into being out of nothing?"

"Nothing?" the voice thundered again. "*Nothing* is an empty word. A reality or something else called *nothing* does not exist."

"And the creation of the universe? Did you not create the world out of nothing?"

"I did not create the universe out of nothing. I am all. *All that is, that was, and will ever be.* The 'is,' 'was,' and 'will be' are used in human language. They are constructs fashioned by human beings for practical purposes. Human life would be a world of chaos without a system of seconds, minutes, hours, days, months and years; past, present, and future; before and after; and so forth. This artificial system does not apply to me. There are no gaps of any kind in the whole scheme of being, and there is no room for *nothing* or for anything else. Would I be god if nothing was next to me, with me, or a rival to me?

"But creativity seems to imply nothing. To *create* is to bring into the world something that did not exist before its creation. Second, can we speak of existence if we do not assume the existence of nothing, or of non-existence? Does the inventor invent something that existed before or something that did not exist before it was invented? Did you create this amazing universe? How?"

"You must have been thinking meditatively about me. First, I did not create the world out of nothing. It has always existed and will continue to exist because I am eternal. Accordingly, because I am an eternal being, it will eternally coexist with me. When I said that creativity is a defining aspect of my being, you should understand creation in terms of emanation—the way light rays emanate from your sun. The universe is an emanation from the depth of my infinite being. The fountain of my creative essence, which is pure light and nothing but light, is an ongoing flow from this depth."

"Does the light come from what already exists or from nothing?" I asked with some hesitation.

"Neither the concept of existence nor the concept of *nothing* applies to me, because the depth of my creative *essence* is a creative *process* of eternal creation. It is an infinite wealth of being. The finite mind does not possess the intellectual categories by which it can understand, much less comprehend the inner logic and dynamics of this depth."

"Does this apply to human creation? Does the artist, inventor, or scientist *create*?"

"Yes, but only from the standpoint of the human intellect. The infinite depth is the source of meaning. You should always remember that the human intellect is, indeed, finite."

"But not from your standpoint?" I asked.

The voice chuckled, and to tell the truth, its chuckle thundered as loudly and frightfully as his angry chuckle had sounded earlier.

"Nothing human beings create, created, or will create escapes the eye of the creative depth of the infinite. What is the finite to the infinite? Where does the artist, the scientist, and the inventor derive their inspiration, vision, and substance of their work but from reflecting on a fraction of the inexhaustible depth of *my* being? This depth is the reason for being—not only of human beings but also of everything they produce."

"But how can we think of existence without thinking of or implying non-existence? Can I say 'exist' without implying that it might or might not exist? What does it mean to say, 'X exists' if non-existence, or *nothing*, does not exist from the standpoint of human beings?"

"You should make a distinction between existence as a *logical* category and existence as an *ontological* category. When you say, 'X exists,' you are making an assertion on the basis of what you experience, of course in the present, and you make this statement to contradistinguish it from the existence of other objects in your perceptual field. On the other hand, when you say, 'X does not exist,' assuming that it refers to an object that exists, you should mean that it does not exist here but somewhere else. You cannot say 'X does not exist' if X does not *actually* exist somewhere. Otherwise, you would be talking about a fictitious object that exists in somebody's mind only."

"If you did not, or do not, create the universe from nothing," I pressed, "if you are an eternal process of emanation from the depth of your being? If an essential aspect of your being is conversation, *in what sense* is the universe *qua* emanation a conversation? A speech act? Not a human conversation but an ontological process or event that makes this universe possible or a reality?"

"You should not ask about what the human mind cannot comprehend," the voice rumbled.

"If I can ask," I replied, "no matter the object of my question, the power of asking must have been given, or at least inspired, by you. I might not be able to comprehend the meaning or answer to my question, but I would like to understand. I am seeking to understand the ultimate ground of my being, and I desire to stand on this ground."

"Then, you should understand what I shall say metaphorically. Otherwise, you shall remain in the dark for the rest of your life."

"I comprehend what you say."

"The infinite depth that I am is not a static but an infinitely dynamic wealth of light. The essence of this wealth is conversation—a dialogue between and among the good, the better, and always the best as an ideal, as a potentiality, and as the means of realizing it as light. Although in its essence, it is rational, nevertheless, its realization is a struggle. A delicious struggle, I should add."

"The ideal?" I blurted out foolishly.

"I am the ideal and I am the real," the voice thundered and then added, "and I am the struggle. This is my nature. Do not let your imagination go wild into some silly anthropomorphism. Reflect on what I say as a model of thinking, of explaining something that surpasses the possibility of thinking, understanding, and comprehension."

"Then the infinite depth of your being is an everlasting fountain of creation."

"Your inference is valid."

"But if it is an infinite depth of creation, does it expand in magnitude in the infinite aspects of your being?" I asked.

"It is an infinite source of space, time, thought, and every conceivable aspect. But the infinite is not amenable to quantification, because it is infinite by its very essence; the infinite is not quantifiable, not by human categories."

"If the creative essence of your depth is conversation, and if this conversation is an *endeavor,* a delicious struggle, as you say, what are the elements of this conversation, or struggle? In a conversation, I converse with myself or with someone else. In a struggle, there are forces that stand in opposition to each other. Is there a hint of an analogy between this kind of conversation and the struggle that you live and human conversation and struggle?

"Live?" the voice thundered. "I do not live. I *am.* Creation is a mode of my being. Analogies, especially in relation to me, can be very misleading. Do not slip into anthropomorphism!"

"Because you are a conversation, and because struggle is one of your essential aspects, can we say that you are *imperfect*? Or that you create what you do not have?"

"You are gliding deeper into anthropomorphism," the voice rumbled. "Although I reveal myself in my creation, the infinite depth that I am transcends my creation. The ideal that I am and the real that I am transcend what I am because the two give continual birth to each other. Categories such as deficiency, imperfection, and striving are superfluous. They and similar categories are conceptual constructs. These constructs are derived from human experience and apply to human beings but not to me."

"How can you be transcendent and immanent at the same time?""

You should be able to answer this question," the voice rumbled. "I am transcendent in the sense that I am an infinite depth and so surpasses the capacity of the human mind conceive me. This is why some of my lovers have characterized me as the ineffable, the unspeakable, or the absolute. But I am also immanent in the sense that the universe, one of my emanations, reveals certain aspects of my being. Why should you find it strange if someone tells you that the fountain of all creation can reveal itself in what it creates? Does the artist not reveal herself in what she creates? Does the human being not reveal herself in her actions? Can you allow this to the artist or the ordinary human being but not to the power that created the artist, the ordinary human being, and everything that exists?"

This last response by the voice was followed by sublime silence. The commotion, which diverted my attention away from the world and everything in it, was replaced by serene calm. The stuffy air I breathed when I was tumbling into the cave was replaced by a wave of fresh air, and the anxiety, fear, and confusion that overwhelmed me before and during the conversation was replaced by a feeling of inner harmony and peace. I felt secure. I felt at home!

It might seem odd, dear reader, if I tell you that when I regained my normal consciousness, immediately following this conversation, I found myself in the same spot and in the same position I was in when I tumbled into the cave. I felt like I had just woken up from a deep sleep or reverie. I looked around to see where I was. The cave was empty but not of life because its walls, ceiling, air, and ground were pulsating with a pure, ethereal, indescribable dynamism. Although the voice stopped speaking, and silence prevailed, every word it said was ingrained in my mind.

What the infinite depth says can never be forgotten. I felt the presence of those words. They were not abstractions, oh no, they were living drops of meaning, light, and power. I felt them the way you feel the crackles of a raging fire in your hearth in a cold winter night. But I was unable to reflect on the meaning and implications of those words because the fatigue that had settled in my muscles during the day and the hunger that was nagging my stomach prompted me to inspect my surroundings and find an appropriate place to spend the night.

The cave was a complex of a few minor caverns. They were illuminated by the same light that had lit the cavern when I was having my conversation with the voice. In one of them, I found a small cataract flowing into a pond. The water of the pond was passing through an opening into the mountain. I smiled when I stood before that waterfall. I looked around. Alas—not a stir! The only sound I heard was that of the running water. Involuntarily, I placed my knapsack on the floor and took a bath in the pond, filled my canteens with water, and ate my evening meal. Life crawled into my veins.

"That was him," I thought to myself, awed. "That was god the infinite! He spoke to me without speaking, understood me without understanding, and felt with me without feeling me! Did he lead me away from that fatal slide into the cave? Was he watching over me when I was climbing those tortuous precipices and steep elevations? Did he save me from tripping into the soft gravel on those ledges and mountain sides? He must have, for how could I have survived that fatal slide without his help? Yes! I must be in safe hands!"

These and a swarm of other questions made their way into my mind when I was eating my supper. Then I sat on the edge of the pond and contemplated the falling water. I did not allow those questions to cloud my vision of the ultimate object of my passion: *to have a union with the author of the voice.* I wanted to move from the edge to the bosom of the depth, to the fire that gives rise to every sun and every ray of light that did or will emanate from it. I wished to see—to experience—what it was like to sit in his lap and suck the nectar of being from his breast and listen to the music of his heartbeats. Music spoke to my soul. I wished to hear the melody of all melodies. Oh, how I wish to exist and flourish from the depth of that melody!

My heart swelled with passion, and my passion was on fire! It was not the passion of desire, of hope, of anticipation, or of wish. "How could it be any of these if I heard his voice, if I spoke with it, and if it blessed me with its answers?" I thought. "I cannot return to the land of human civilization unless I have this union with him, unless I suck a few drops of that nectar. No power can deter me from satiating this all-embracing passion."

Chapter Seven

The Fluteplayer's Last Conversation with God

I DO not recall how I slept, if I ever did, that night after my conversation with the voice. It seems to me that the flow of time that constitutes the inner structure of my inner being was never interrupted. That night was, in some mysterious way, erased from my memory bank. All I remember is that I was standing at the doorstep of a new day. I soon discovered that that moment marked my second, and I should say *real* birth—the birth of my new character, my new life, and my new destiny.

The same volcanic voice that had arrested my consciousness and the world around me when I tumbled into the cave the evening before thundered again that morning. Like it had before, the voice quaked the cave and the ground on which I was sleeping. Frightened, I opened my eyes to a flood of light that seemed to emanate from that thundering voice. It might seem strange if I say that I was not aware of anything at all except light, pure light. I stood in it, I felt its warmth, and I breathed from that warmth!

"You did not leave!" the voice thundered without giving me a chance to collect myself.

"No, I did not leave, I cannot leave, and I have no desire to leave!" I said.

"You are a determined and courageous man," the voice said. "Why have you lingered in this cave?"

"To hear your voice thunder, to enjoy the music of this thunder, and to learn—"

"You do not need to be poetic with me," the voice interrupted with an explosive thunderbolt. All metaphors, figures of speech, and symbols stand naked before my ears. I do not hear your words, I hear the pulse of your mind and feel the fire that sparkles in your heart. This pulse and these sparkles are the language I hear, and this is the language I understand. State your purpose!"

"I have a bundle of questions."

"Commence!"

"Why do I exist rather than not?" I asked with a quiver in my voice.

"I answered this question yesterday. It was implied in my explanation of *the why* and the *mode of existence* of my being."

"It eluded my understanding. I need your help."

"Let me begin with a new formulation of the question: why do I, the *I* that embraces you, the universe and the infinity of my being, exist?"

"Yes please!" I cried.

"This way of formulating the question is a bad—and I should add a logically wrongheaded—and incorrect way of formulating it."

"Why?"

"Because it springs from the doctrine of causation that rests on the necessary relation between cause and effect. Everything that exists, be it an object or an event, must have a cause. Accordingly, if I exist, I must have a cause. But this doctrine is deficient—"

"Why?" I interrupted rather impulsively.

"It applies to the things that make up the fabric of the universe but not to me as the *absolute being than which nothing greater can be conceived and nothing greater than which can exist.*"

"Can you explain this point, please?"

"If you imply the existence of such a being, one that can be conceived and one that actually exists, it should, according to the doctrine of causation, have a cause. But then, you can justifiably ask for the cause of this second cause that is supposed to be superior to me, and so on infinitely! But this progression or regression is absurd, and it is absurd not only according to my logic, which is infinitely superior to yours, but also according to your own logic. You should always remember that the concept of cause and effect, which was articulated and defended by the early philosophers and then by the scientists, is the most effective way of explaining natural and human phenomena.

"The human mind cannot conceive a better or a higher principle—one that explains the phenomena that transcend the universe and everything finite in it. They speak of infinity, the absolute, the boundless, or the ultimate. But do they conceive, much less comprehend, their significations? They speculate and theorize on the transcendent irresponsibly. Do you not think that you can create numerous and frequently conflicting and contradictory theories and conceptions about what you cannot experience or even conceive?

"The history of your civilization is littered with these theories and conceptions. Then again, the philosophers boldly claim that a judgment is sound inasmuch as it is corroborated by facts. But the infinite is not a fact of experience, at least not directly. How can they make a sound judgment about its nature or existence? Now, if your reasoning begins with the premise that the infinite is beyond your experience and comprehension and grant that he transcends the universe, then you cannot ask for a being that created me. For if you do, then you assume that I am not the infinitely absolute being.

"Even according to your logic, the concept of absolute being implies that no higher being can be conceived to exist next to, with, or against me. Therefore, it would be a grave mistake to ask who created me or if there is a being superior to me. And from my point of view, I am neither the cause of nor superior to anything! I am I, and I am an eternal emanation of light from the infinite depth, which is me. Words such as 'transcendent,' 'superior,' 'god,' and 'absolute,' which you tend to use interchangeably, are human constructs; they reveal the inability of the human mind to comprehend what lies beyond its experience. Do you follow this line of reasoning?"

"I do, and I understand what you say. But this line of reasoning does not seem to apply, at least at first look, to my question, that is, to all the finite objects in the universe. Maybe it does, but I am not certain."

"Why do you express this doubt?"

"You are you, and you are eternal; but I am not. As far as I know, nothing in the universe is. I come into existence at one moment in time and pass out of existence at another moment. This applies to every object that exists in the universe. The law that rules the cosmic process is the law of perishing. Why should this king dominate the cosmic process? Why should I be born if I shall die soon, especially after I taste the meaning of existence, of life, and if I am smitten by the delicious fire of the sun that illuminates the world? What baffles my mind is that if you are eternal, and if I and everything in the universe is an emanation of your being, why should I perish? I do not know whether the rock, the lion, or the rose plant is aware of its impending perishing, or whether it is concerned about it, but I and human beings, in general, are. I seek understanding."

"You speak as a moralist. This is good but not enough. You think as a human being and you use moral values as a basis for evaluating the question of existence and perishing. But when you think metaphysically, and in the right way, the mystic's way, you think from my standpoint. Think from my standpoint."

"How?"

"The process of emanation, and here I intend the emanation that flows from the depth of my being, is a process of permanent creation: it is creative activity. Struggle is, as I pointed out earlier, one of its essential aspects. As an eternal emanation, I am the *vital impetus* of all being, and I am the power that sustains it. This impetus originates from and is one with the depth of my infinite being. Without its effort, the universe and everything in it would collapse into total darkness. Now, if you focus your imagination on the universe as an emanation, you will discover, by necessity, that the cosmic process, *or the universe as a luminous emanation, is a creative activity*. Its supreme aim is the good. As an ideal, the ideal is not real but a possibility for becoming real. The activity of realizing it, of making it a living emanation, involves effort—struggle.

"But you should not think of this struggle anthropomorphically or from the standpoint of subjective desire or interest but objectively, metaphysically. What might seem good or beautiful to you is not necessarily good or beautiful in itself, even though you might judge it as so. I should here emphasize an important fact: the creative process in all the spheres of being, even in the sphere of infinity, aims at the good and the beautiful. This process is never smooth, otherwise, there would not be any struggle in realizing the good and the beautiful. But if it is not smooth, then there will be discordance, destruction, and different types of failures. It is easy for a human being to view and interpret these types of evil from her moral standpoint and evaluate it on the basis of her moral values. If she does this, she will commit what you very well know as the *ego-centric fallacy*."

"Does this mean that moral values such as justice, love, friendship, honesty, to mention a few of them, all of which people prize and seek to realize in their individual and social lives, are not objectively valid? Is their pursuit subjective, arbitrary, or expedient in nature? Some people, not many, are willing to die for them. Are they justified in their unwavering adherence to them? And, as a corollary to this question, if they are valid, or valid to some extent, what makes them valid? The last question arises from a long and deep reflection on the nature and meaning of human life as it has revealed itself during the past five thousand years.

"It is not easy to truly live according to these values in a world that is not hospitable to them socially and naturally. The few people who have reached a reasonable degree of spiritual achievement, who care about the well-being of their souls, who understand the meaning of human life and destiny—yes, those people know that living according to these values necessarily entails denial of all the pleasures, power, wealth, and glory of this world. They also know that they have to struggle and suffer plenty of frustration and pain, and they know that they will be alienated, mocked and frequently oppressed by others, even by their family members and sometimes by their neighbors and colleagues. Are these people wise in pursuing this way of life if they know, and they certainly know, that their lives are short, and that they will soon pass into the world of eternal oblivion?"

"There was no need to explain your question dramatically, although the predicament you have described is dramatic from your standpoint."

"I am human and so I cannot express myself in any other way."

"Yes!" the voice rumbled, but this time compassionately. "These values are valid inasmuch as they originate from my nature or, to use a simpler language, from my will."

"But I have always thought that they are valid inasmuch as they originate from the essence of human nature."

"Your thinking is correct inasmuch as your understanding of human nature originates from or is true to the light that emanates from my being. No value, idea, or principle of action is valid if it does not originate from this light. My will is the ultimate source and standard of truth, goodness, and beauty. Accordingly, a human being who lives according to these values is an authentic being."

"And we can say that she lives according to your will?"

"Certainly."

"But why should such a being lead an authentic life is if it is going to be vitiated with painful struggle, alienation, and frequently loneliness, and especially if she knows that she and her life is no more than a passing ripple in the cosmic process? It is good and morally obligatory to live authentically, but why? Is it because these values originate from your will? I grant that you are their source: should I adhere to them because they are *intrinsically* true, simply because they originate from your will, or simply because you are god?"

"Because they are true, absolutely true—true in themselves, because their truth shines from within, not from without!"

"And they are intrinsically true because they originate from your will?"

"Yes!" the voice rumbled. "You should live according to them because they are true, not simply because they originate from my will or simply because I am god. Yes, they are intrinsically true because I am their source and because I am the only god. There is not another authority, one that surpasses me in wisdom, power, and goodness, that can be such a source. Let me express this point differently: you should live according to them because they are intrinsically true, and because I am their source: they are true because I am god, and I am god because I am the ultimate measure of the true, the good, and the beautiful. If I were not such a measure, I would not be god! I am the truth and the source of all truth! Thus, you should not live according to them out of fear but because I am the source of the truth. If you live according to them out of fear or simply because I am god, your life will not be authentic."

"But does the fact that they originate from your will *create an obligation* to live according to them?"

"You and you alone should answer this question. No one should answer it for you."

"Why?"

"Can you live in darkness after you see the light? Can you live in ignorance after you *discover* your ignorance? Can you live alone after your heart is smitten by the fire of love? Can you live in bondage after you breathe the air of freedom? The answer to your question cannot be dictated by an external authority; it should originate freely from your will, from your understanding of the human and natural worlds from the standpoint of their source. In short, from inner conviction. The central question any human being should face is whether she is willing to be authentic—that is, whether she is willing to base her life-project on these three values. A person who lives according to them will frown upon all the pain, all the alienation, and all the loneliness she faces."

"Is it human, is it possible to frown upon these evils?"

"If a human being aims at joy, and if this joy comes from living an authentic life, she will certainly frown upon them. What is the experience of joy compared to the experience of alienation, pain, or loneliness? The question is not to live as a lump of flesh but as a *human being*! The first is easy, but the second is not! But it is more difficult, *much* more difficult, for a person who knows the meaning of joy, who drank a cup of it, to live as a lump of flesh!"

"Even when she knows that she will soon fade into the world of eternal oblivion—sooner than she can imagine?"

"Yes!"

"Why?"

"Because every flicker, every achievement, every creative action she performs *is intrinsically valuable.* A human being is *real* inasmuch as she is authentic, and she is authentic inasmuch as she lives from the human flame in her heart. An inauthentic life is a life of deception—a lie. An individual who knows what it means to be a human being but declines to live according to the essential demands of humanity is, at the human level, a very poor, if not a dead being. She does not have to await her death at some time in the future. She might survive at the biological or social level the way many people do, but is this way of life worth living? Do you wish to live in order to survive *biologically or socially* or as a *human being*?"

"But my fellow human beings who are oblivious to these values, who pay lip service to them, or who do not understand why they exist—in short, those who are committed to the pursuit of fame, pleasure, power, wealth, and knowledge—would mock a person who seeks and in fact struggles to lead an authentic life. Mr. Everyman would stare her in the face and say, 'You are a foolish person. You are denying yourself the pleasures of life and instead you are leading a life of struggle, anxiety, frustration, and pain. You seem to live like a blind person who does not know where she is going or what she is doing. You cannot even see that at the end of the line, there is one thing and one thing only: death!

"You are an intelligent human being. *Think!* Your life is short. You will soon die, and you will not relive it. Why should you lead a life of misery, loneliness, and pain? Why do you not enjoy it—ha? Do not underestimate Everyman's way of life. Life is sweet, sweet to the core. Why should you deny yourself the sweetness of pleasure? Delight in it as long as you can and for as long as you can. Do not be a foo! Is Everyman foolish or wise? The question that disturbs every person who endeavors to lead an authentic life is that if Everyman's advice to me contains some, even a speck, of truth, perhaps wisdom, then would a seeker of these values be under any obligation to seek them? If so, how? Would such an obligation be justifiable? But what if it is justifiable?"

"These values," the voice thundered, and its thunder pierced through my eardrums, "are justifiable!"

"What makes them justifiable?"

"You seem to forget what I said earlier. My word is the ultimate principle of justifying the truth of these values. It is the standard of all standards in evaluating the truth of any idea or value in any theoretical or practical sphere of human experience. My word is this principle because there is not, and there will never be, a higher principle. Remember: I am the absolute!"

"I understand every word you say, but—" I faltered.

"But what?" the thundering voice asked and waited for an answer.

"Is it justifiable for Everyman to deprive himself of the pleasures of life if he will soon step into the world of eternal oblivion?"

"If these values are justifiable, and they are, pursuing them at any cost, no matter how hard it might be, is justifiable."

"And is depriving oneself of the pleasures of life justifiable? Are you not the author of everything? Can anything you create or allow be bad?"

"Before you try to answer this question, let me ask you: is the struggle, pain, frustration, and loneliness, in short, the suffering one experiences and frequently *lives* in her pursuit of these values not sweeter than the pursuit of pleasure? Is the genuine experience of real beauty, goodness, and truth not more satisfying than a lifetime of pleasure? But what is *ironic* is that a life devoted to the pursuit of pleasure is not as easy as many pleasure seekers tend to think it is; it is frequently a source of deep and lasting frustration, which creates an undercurrent of *continual anxiety*."

"Why?" I asked impatiently.

"Because the feeling of pleasure is a highly superficial feeling; it is a *surface feeling* that does not satisfy what the mind and the heart desire. Moreover, pleasure is a short-lived experience. It lasts as long its source lasts. The moment the source ceases to exist, the feeling of pleasure ends; and when it ends one feels empty and frequently disappointed. This feeling creates an urge to look for another source, and the process is endless. This kind of life is similar to the life of a grasshopper that constantly hops from one plant to another! But on the other hand, one moment of living the good, the true, or the beautiful is a never-ending fountain of satisfaction.

"I do not exaggerate if I emphasize that such a moment is more satisfying than all the pleasures Everyman seems to enjoy or claims to enjoy. Do you not feel fulfilled when you help a fellow human being in distress, discover a philosophical or scientific truth about nature or the magnificent drama of human life as it has been progressing in the course of history? Do such experiences not become integral and constructive parts of your thinking and feeling mechanisms in your life? Do you not feel, when this happens, the *rhythm of human growth pulsating* in every fiber of your being? But on the other hand, can you even remember most of the pleasurable experiences you have had in the near and distant past? Yes, you do remember some of them, often when they spring directly from the flame of your heart or when the pleasure is associated with such experiences.

"I am sure that the question of whether it is your obligation to live according to the three central values is lurking actively in the back of your mind. If it moves to the front and stares you in the face, ignore it! As I emphasized to you earlier, make your own decisions and always be content with them. This contentment must come from within, for your mind and will! In matters of right and wrong or good and bad, neither I nor any power of your universe can or should assume responsibility for your decisions. The moment you surrender this responsibility to an external authority, you also surrender your dignity! The question is 'to be or not to be.' The answer to this question is, of course, to be; but can you *be* if your life does not flow from your heart? *Can you be* if you lead the life of a slave? Can you be if you dim the human flame that kindles in your heart—?"

"How can I make any kind of decision if I am a creature?" I said, interrupting the voice. "I was born without my knowledge and choice, and I shall die also without my knowledge and choice. My body was given to me; I did not choose it. My mind and my faculty of desire were also given to me. Moreover, I did not choose my culture, and I did not choose the beliefs and values that make up its fabric. Moreover, I *discovered* myself around the peak of my adolescence; I *discovered* that I am a member in a certain family, society, and state, and that I am obligated to obey their norms and law and observe their customs and traditions. In short, I am a *finite being*. I feel that I am a marionette controlled in my inner and outer life by external forces, and when I reflect on this situation deeply, I feel that you control my life and the totality of my social and natural environment."

"Yes," the voice rumbled but this time with a shade of solemnity, "you are a creature and are finite in the sense you explained, but you are free, free as a lark that soars into the highest skies of being. I do not exaggerate if I tell you that you are an expressive drop of freedom."

"How can a drop of finitude be a drop of explosive freedom? How can it create anything *ex nihilo*? How can a finite being transcend its finitude? How can it create anything if every element of its being is created?"

"You are an emanation of my being; as such, you are an image of the fire that gave rise to this emanation—"

"An image?" I cried hastily.

The voice rumbled and thundered. "You are an image of the fire that flames in my heart, and you are an extension of this fire. All of the elements that constitute the structure of your being are no more than dwellings of this flame. You are not your body; you are this flame. This flame is the seat of consciousness that thinks, feels, and wills in you; it is the subject that steers your life-project and every action you perform. It is the source of the feelings of love, hope, enthusiasm, and satisfaction and also the source of sadness, frustration, guilt, and loneliness. The flame you are is an explosive drop of freedom because it is an explosive drop of creativity—*ex nihilo*!"

"But how can it exercise its creative power in a world of necessity?"

"The world you live in is not a world of necessity; it is a dynamic reality—a process. Matter, life, norms, laws, ideas, and everything else are in constant change, ultimately for the better. Focus your attention on the history of your civilization. What is the source of the myriad of progressive changes that underlie the whole historical process *but* the power of the vision, passion, devotion, intellectual acuity, and understanding of creative minds in the sphere of science, mathematics, philosophy, art, government, and social reform? Did the scientist submit to the beliefs or laws of the church when he discovered the laws of motion or gravity? Did the engineer submit to the solidity of the different rocks when she tried to build roads, extract minerals, or did she subjugate them to his will? Did the social reformer submit her will to the despot or the corrupt government, or did she discover ways to change their ways? In short, can any law, voice, or power stop you from believing what you think is true or good?"

"But how many lives were sacrificed at the altar of injustice, stupidity, vanity, selfishness, exploitation, and ignorance? The history of our humanity is littered with human waste—of destruction! Why? I fully understand your emphasis on certain individuals who upheld the principles of goodness, beauty, and truth and faced the forces of darkness courageously and in some cases, even died for them, but these were few. I aver that they are outstanding exemplifications of creativity. And how about the large masses of human beings who perished and continue to perish without even knowing that they were emanations from your being. Were they explosive drops of creativity, too?"

"You are an observer of the history of civilization—good! Let me first say that the flame that is the foundation of their being, and which is an emanation from my being, is a drop of creativity and so of freedom. Flames can dim or kindle in the human heart. This is a feature of finitude. The life of a human being is a reflection of the light that shines from this flame. It is an explosive drop of creativity. This drop is a *suis generis* source; it does not derive its inner power from an external source but from its inner resources. It can initiate an action on the basis of what it thinks, feels, and wills. In short, it is an independent source of action and therefore, of life.

"Accordingly, it would be a mistake to say that reason is *a power* or source of freedom; it cannot be this kind of power if the faculties of willing and feeling are not equal powers. Can reason make a choice or initiate an action without the responsive cooperation of the will and the emotions? Is it not reasonable to say that they, too, are powers? But how or what endows them with this power? Let me suggest to you that reason, will, and emotion derive their dynamic natures from the flame that sits at the base of the human heart. This flame is an explosive drop of power!

"This drop manifests itself through the work or activity of reason, will, and emotion; it is the ultimate source of the creative vision that opens up new dimensions of meaning in art, philosophy, science, and the practical sphere of human life. Reason is the eyes of the creative process, will is its moving force, and emotion is the hand that transforms the vision into reality. Yes, you can make decisions and implement them. Is rational activity, or the pursuit of knowledge and wisdom, beauty, or the pursuit of art and goodness, or the pursuit of happiness possible *if the human being is not free?*

"Again, can you arrive at the truth of any proposition, theory, or principle if the activity of establishing the truth is dictated by someone? Or if it is constricted by some natural or human handicap? Can the artist create an artwork if she is prevented from choosing an appropriate symbolic form in the process of expression? Can you realize your happiness if someone dictates your way of life? The essence of the human flame is freedom! The capacity of making decisions is the defining feature of this freedom. Now, let me remind you that decision-making is always the making of a plan for a particular course of action. When this plan relates to the individual's life, it becomes a life-project; when it relates to government, it becomes a law or a policy; and when it relates to social life, it becomes a mode of behavior.

"Now, throw an investigative glance at the history of human society and aim at the force that underlies it development. What is the loudest cry of the genuine legislator, the political leader, the philosopher, the scientist, the social reformer, and the individual human being in the pursuit of her happiness or the public good *but a cry for freedom* for the creation of the social, economic, and political conditions under which people can live from the light of the flame that shines in their hearts? Do you not hear this cry coming for the depth your own consciousness when you ascend the mount of your adolescence? Do you not hear it loudly and clearly whenever you encounter an oppressed, disenfranchised, or poor community? Do you not hear it bursting from the pages of your history books when you contemplate the mystery of human life?"

"But what does it mean for a human being to be free?" I asked. "The capacity of decision-making is, as you explained, the defining feature of freedom. How would you characterize the life of a free person?"

"Human freedom does not merely signify mere *freedom from* natural and moral laws. On the contrary, it presupposes them; they are the medium within which freedom is achieved. Freedom in a social and natural vacuum is not freedom. The factors that constrict freedom are ignorance, hate, poverty, prejudice, closed-mindedness, and dogmatism. But human freedom is not only freedom from these and similar obstacles but *freedom to make the right decision* and act on it in a particular social context. This type of decision-making and action is the essence of human freedom. A person is free inasmuch as her life issues from enlightened decision-making in the different domains of human life *as a human being.* Accordingly, the ultimate goal of enlightened decision-making is a *fulfilled life*, one in which the inner demands of human nature—aesthetic, political, social, physical, and intellectual—are met.

"But because the natural, human, and social worlds are dynamic and in general progressive, human fulfillment is always an ongoing process of realization—that is, of growth and development. You should always remember that meeting the essential demands of humanity is never perfect. Human fulfillment, and therefore human freedom, is always relative to the cultural environment in which the individual thrives. Accordingly, the substance of freedom is different from one culture to another. An enlightened decision is made in terms of the material and social resources available to the individual. You cannot choose a course of action or pursue your life-project if it cannot be realized in the particular cultural environment in which you live. Consequently, you cannot evaluate the extent of your freedom in relationship to past or different cultural contexts. Again, you should not view the laws of the state or the beliefs, values, norms, and traditions that make up the texture of your culture as external impositions but as the medium in which you pursue your life-project.

"Spiritually, you are the child of your culture; you derive your sense of value and your understanding of the meaning of life and destiny from its beliefs and values. Overstepping the boundaries of one's culture is no more possible than overstepping the Atlantic Ocean with your legs. Given a particular social context, how can you maximize your growth and development as a human being? Does this mean submitting one's will to the laws of nature or to the moral laws? No. It only means striving for realizing the greatest possibilities implicit in them."

"But what if these laws or norms are unjust, unbearably oppressive?"

"This is a question of social or moral activism, not of the meaning of freedom and the conditions under which it can be realized. The history of your civilization is dotted with admirable examples of social, political, and moral activism. It always aimed at *securing* the conditions under which human beings can be free or freer."

"There are two types of social activism—peaceful and violent. When is a person or a group justified in voicing *active* objection to bad laws?"

"Only when it is certain that these laws undermine the realization of the public good. Laws are instruments of social and moral progress; they are justifiable inasmuch as they serve the wellbeing of society, and they are unjustifiable inasmuch as they are harmful to society. Prevention of harm is a moral obligation; it is the principle that justifies social activism."

"How can we define *social good*?"

"It is defined in terms of freedom. Any law, practice, project, policy, or action that constricts the moral and social progress of the individual or society is morally deficient, or bad. It is crucially important to make sure that before you initiate any objection to a moral law or policy, that the law or policy actually restricts the freedom of the individual or society. It is equally important to articulate a morally acceptable alternative to the existing law or policy. To be successful, the objection must command the understanding and approval of the pubic."

"What if the public is mired in apathy or ignorance?"

"The only power that justifies objection to any type of law or policy is rational persuasion, not violence. A bad law or policy should be changed *rationally and by legal means*. Violence breeds violence. In itself, violence is evil; evil is not conducive to good results. It might be conducive to some good in the short but not in the long run."

"What if the existing legal and social situation is intolerable? What if a few people are able to change the existing situation by violent means? Is this type of action morally justifiable? Would these few, or sometimes even one person, be justified in *remaining silent*?"

"First, the few or the one should do their utmost to change the situation rationally—by legal or peaceful means."

"What if these means fail? As you can see, I am anxious to arrive at a principle that can be the basis of solving moral deficiency or conflict in recalcitrant situations. Such situations do not occur only in the public sphere but also in the family, work, religious, and personal spheres."

"I see the source of your anxiety. There is no need to explain your concern to me," the voice rumbled, but this time sympathetically. "The good triumphs and should always triumph. The existence of evil in the universe is sometime necessary but neither always nor absolutely. On the whole, it exists for a reason, and the reason is promotion of good."

"Whose good?" I interrupted impulsively.

"The highest good."

"The highest good?" I exclaimed involuntarily.

"Yes, not the good of this group, individual, or society, but the true good. A perception of this good in a particular situation originates from an intuition of the highest good. The moral judgment should be an articulation of this intuition. In some situations, violence might be justifiable, but in others (and hopefully in most of the others), it is not. A judgment founded on this type of intuition does not stem from a violent mind and can never perform or tolerate violent action. It views violence as a necessary last resort."

"Is this an oblique way of justifying violence?"

"This is a clear, honest way of acknowledging the reality of what you call *evil* in the universe. The question of evil is inescapable in the human world. The forces of good should combat and obstruct its activity and dominance."

"Why?"

"In a world of perfection, the question of evil does not arise. It arises in the human world because it is finite. Deficiency is an essential aspect of finitude. We have already discussed this question."

"Yes, we have. I understand the logical thread of your explanation. But if deficiency is an essential aspect of finitude; if the good should triumph, at least in human life; if struggle is an ingredient in the realization of the good; if human beings who are committed to the cause of the good frequently suffer severe pain and sometimes death in pursuing good; and finally; if you see and know everything that happens in the universe, because it is an emanation of your being, *do you care* about the destructive presence of evil in the world? Do you *sympathize* with those who suffer in their endeavors to promote the good? Do you *feel* a desire to help them? In short, *do you love?*"

The sympathetic rumble the voiced fired at me earlier was transmuted into a volcanic flash of thunder. "Anthropomorphism again!" it bellowed. "Anthropomorphism is a trap. Avoid this trap! I am the source of all the types of love that exist in the human world and everywhere in the infinity of being."

"I seek understanding," I said, interrupting the voice.

"I know. The essence of the loving act is giving, not receiving, a kind of good. The loving feature of the loving human being is the inherent tendency of the individual to do good and refrain from doing evil. The majority of people in your society define love in terms of what they receive. For them, you are good and loving inasmuch as you give them, not inasmuch as they give to you. They treat interest as the standard by which they evaluate acts of goodness or love. Do not forget that love is the essence of goodness. Whether it is in the family, the workplace, or social interactions, the strong as well as the weak define good on the basis of what they receive. The strong tend to define it in terms of laws, rules, and policies, and the weak tend to define it in terms of gratitude, flattery, submissive reaction, and gesture. But although the weak are the majority, your society is blessed with many genuine lovers. What is it that prompts the scientist, the philosopher, the social reformer, the benevolent leader, the teacher, the parent, the friend, and many other human beings who walk unnoticed in the streets of social life to deny themselves most if not all of the privileges, glories, wealth, power, and pleasures of the world *and aim at the good first and foremost? Such people are fountains of giving.* They are true lovers, and they are creative people *par excellence.* Let me here remark that the creative act is always *a creative act* primarily because it is constructive act. The good it produces is a novel reality. It is an event in which the ideal of the good steps into the real world. Loving people are smitten by the fire the sun. They live from that fire and walk in its light.

"A good heart is always a feeling heart. The impetus to love necessarily generates, a warm feeling of approval which, in turn, generates a feeling of satisfaction when one performs a loving act, regardless of whether its recipient is a family member, a friend, a neighbor, or an unknown person. And yet, the loving act cannot be defined by the feeling or emotion it arouses or that which prompts it; on the contrary, the activity of giving that originates from a good heart is what justifies the arousal of the emotion or the feeling of approbation. An act acquires its moral character from the fact that it originates freely from a good heart. This type of heart is a source of love."

"Do you love your human creation in this sense of love?"

"If I do not have a human body and mind, can I love the way human beings love?" the voice thundered. "But again, how can the fountain of the infinity of being, including humanity, love the way human beings do?"

"But the founders of the major religions and the faithful in these religions view you and relate to you as a loving being, as a father, as a mother, as merciful, as a responsive being. How should we understand them when they characterize you in any of these and similar ways?"

"If they think I am a mega-human being or humanity writ large, absolutely larger, they are mistaken. All anthropomorphic tendencies in any discourse about me should be dispelled from their minds."

"And the purpose of worship?"

"I did not ask for it! Ask those who created it!"

"We usually feel awe, amazement, and wonder when we stand before a great feat in science, art, philosophy, social reform, or political legislation. It would seem proper, indeed unavoidable, to feel only enthralled, mystified, and overwhelmed by the sublimity, magnificence, and beauty of the universe, by the way it was created, and especially by its creator. Does this act not infinitely surpass in majesty, grandeur, splendor, and depth of meaning anything the human mind can either conceive, comprehend, or create? Human beings feel an insistent desire to express a feeling of appreciation, gratitude, and respect—"

I was unable to complete my sentence because the voice interrupted me in an impatient tone "I do not need the appreciation, adulation, reverence, or gratitude of anyone!"

"I fully understand what you say. Human beings express their respect and appreciation to their heroes and benefactors, but you are the creator of their lives. You have given them the gift of being a part of the cosmic process, and most of all, you have bestowed upon them the honor of living in the light of your presence. At least from their point of view, they feel a need to express how they feel toward you."

"This is a human need. They can meet it in the privacy of their souls and nowhere else."

"How?"

"By promoting the good, the true, and the beautiful in their lives and the lives of their fellow human beings. Living according to these values is

140

the ultimate source of harmony and peace they truly desire. Instead of having faith in an idol they constructed in their image, they should have faith in the dignity, power, light, and majesty of these values. Only when people's lives originate from them as principles of action can they understand the nature of the loving act. Only then can they see what it means for me to be a loving god. Has it occurred to you that these values are the greatest gift the founders of the major religions have given to the world? Human beings truly feel my presence when they see that the beautiful is true and beautiful, that the true is good and beautiful, and that the good is true and good."

I was going to declare to the voice my desire to feel the depth of the infinite from which these values originated, to feel the pulse of the creative act that gives rise to them, and especially, to be baptized by the light that illuminates their essence. And yes, I desired to see these three values in the radiance of their unity in the heart that gave birth to them. But my desire was not fulfilled because the voice suddenly vanished and was followed by the most awesome silence your mind can imagine. I felt its presence in that silence—why not? Is he not immanent in his creation, even in the silence he leaves behind? But the presence his silence left in that cavern was not the presence of an absence: it was pure presence. It was a warm presence, and it was the kind that speaks. The language it spoke at that moment was not the language of silence, human silence, but of faith. Not the faith of the dogmatic, zealous, and intolerant believer who does not know what and why she believes, but the believer who lives from the light that gives rise to her belief. I felt secure, upheld, and at home in the warmth of that silence. I lingered in it for a long time, and I emerged from it the way you emerge from a deep, peaceful sleep.

The first thing I did when I regained my ordinary consciousness was to go to the pond, drink some water, and have a bath. Then I ate a meal and visited the other caverns. They were empty. There was not any trace of human presence in them. Then I went back to the pond and sat on its ledge.

"I must be close to the edge," I thought. The voice spoke to me from the depth, but the depth was my goal, and I was determined to reach my goal. My inmost desire was to stand before the sun, to contemplate the fire that gives rise to the cosmic process, and to see how life flows from it, if possible. Yes, I desired to sit in its lap next to its heart and listen to the melody that gives rise to that process.

I must have spent the whole day thinking in that cave because the voice that thundered into my ears and shook the foundation on the ground on which I was sitting spoke again.

"Why are you still here? You should have left, but you did not—why?" the voice thundered.

I was so frightened when I heard those words, which darted into my ears as an arrow of fire. I stood and faced it the way a child faces her mother when she does something wrong and is about to receive a reprimand. I tried to speak but could not. I needed a few moments to collect myself. Hearing that thundering voice at that point of my journey was an extraordinary happening; it was not easy for me to be calm, confident, or self-composed. However, the voice did not give me a chance to collect myself.

"Speak!" it ordered.

Unable to express myself properly, I blurted out, "I have been in love with you ever since my mind became conscious of its existence and the existence of the world. I have been seeking you all my life. I have been gazing at the sun, and I have been blinded by its light. But the more I gazed at it, the more I was blinded by its light, the more I was determined to be burned by the light of your fire. I love this fire."

"This fire is forbidden to human beings."

"But you cannot forbid your lovers from embracing you."

"I am I, and you are you. Neither your heart nor your mind can embrace me."

"I understand what you say, but my passion to embrace you is wider, deeper, and greater than my mind or heart is. Where did this passion come from but you? Therefore, I am justified in my desire to embrace you."

"You speak correctly."

"Then, let me, please!"

"You cannot endure the fire of my heart."

"I wish to be consumed by it. Roasting in its flame is the only baptism I seek!"

"The consequences might be fatal."

"If I am to die, I wish to die in your lap, within the flames of that fire."

"You are determined?"

"Yes!"

"What makes you sure?"

"You and no one else."

"Then walk through the third cavern and do not look backward or sideward," the voice thundered and vanished.

The ultimate wish of my heart was granted. Without wasting a second, I walked through the first and second caverns and without hesitation moved into the third. The wall that was made of solid rock disappeared and revealed an indefinable vista of brightness. I walked into it.

This is all I can describe, dear reader. Earlier in my memoirs, I frequently appealed to symbols such as the sun, the depth, the light, the infinite, and the absolute to communicate my ideas and feelings of what I experienced, but the experience I underwent—and even the word "experience" should be understood metaphorically in this context—what I experienced after I walked into that brightness defies description by any kind of symbol imaginable by the human mind.

But, alas, if it is indescribable, can it be remembered?
No.

I cannot remember or even conjecture how long I stayed in the land beyond the vista of brightness—where I went, what I did, or what happened to me. The first and only thing I recall soon after I marched into that vista is the moment I reentered the third cavern. It seemed that the event of leaving the cavern and reentering it were continuous but with one exception: I discovered myself singing when I sat at the ledge of the pond. This sudden recognition baffled me because I never sang before I ascended the peakless mountain. But this recognition was only the beginning of an awareness that began to unfold gradually in my mind: I felt like I was a new human being, quite different from the one I was when I marched into that vista of brightness.

Inner peace, one that transcends any social, psychological, or physical peace, reigned supreme in my mind and heart. I felt that the music that was flying from my mouth rose from the depth of that peace. How did I acquire the art of singing? I cannot answer this question, but I confess that my life was thenceforth an endless song. Every desire I felt, every idea I thought, every decision I made, and every action I performed was an echo of that song. I walked on the ground and moved about as I always did, but the ground on which I walked was pliable, almost ethereal—or, could it be that I was pliable, ethereal? I cannot say! The physical world that stood before me as an alien and sometimes hostile reality is now a friendly, hospitable world. I felt like every aspect, every dimension of nature was co-extensive with my being.

A noteworthy change I underwent, one every human being longs for, is a profound feeling of self-control: I was in charge of my thinking, feeling, and willing powers, and more importantly, I was in charge of my destiny. The feeling of apprehension I used to experience when I faced serious challenges and the fear and burden of responsibility that usually accompanied any serious action I performed receded into the farthest recesses of my mind. On the contrary, everything I did proceeded from clear understanding, confident will, and certain expectations without anxiety about the kind of consequences that might ensue from my action. Everything I did proceeded from the inner peace I felt in my heart when I reentered the third cavern.

Descending a high, steep mountain is as difficult as ascending it. But descending the peakless mountain was, contrariwise, easier, much easier than ascending any high, steep mountain. Soon after I reached its foot and traversed the strip of land that separated it from Mountain City, I went directly to the motel from which I had embarked on the adventure of my life. The woman received me, as she had done before, with a smile. Her husband was sitting on the same high chair next to her reading the newspaper.

"How was your trip?" the woman asked. I noticed that her eyes were glued to my face. Although she recognized me, she was scrutinizing me and every movement and gesture I made. She must have discovered something about me she did not see or recognize during my last visit to her motel. Frankly, her eyes glowed with curiosity.

"Excellent! Better than I ever expected!"

"Wonderful! Anything happen to your hair?" she paused for a second and then added. "And your beard is rather long."

Her eyes never left my face. Her husband, who must have noted the strange conversation his wife was having with me, lifted his head off the newspaper and cast a long and curious glance at me. The newspaper he was holding in his hands fell to the ground. He picked it up and gazed into my eyes for a prolonged moment as if he was looking for some hidden message or meaning in them. I responded to his spying gaze with a smile.

"I told you he is one of them loonies!" he said.

"Did you—?" his wife asked her husband in a whispering voice. But I did not hear the rest of her question. Does it matter? There is much in our lives that does not matter!

I went to my room with a contented heart. I did not have any dreams that night. In fact, I never had them for the remainder of my life.

www.ingramcontent.com/pod-product-compliance
Lightning Source LLC
Chambersburg PA
CBHW051838020726
47502CB00005B/1845